KU-610-614

Silver Spurs and Lead

GEORGE J. PRESCOTT

A Black Horse Western

ROBERT HALE · LONDON

© George J. Prescott 2004
First published in Great Britain 2004

ISBN 0 7090 7478 6

Robert Hale Limited
Clerkenwell House
Clerkenwell Green
London EC1R 0HT

The right of George J. Prescott to be identified as
author of this work has been asserted by him
in accordance with the Copyright, Designs and
Patents Act 1988.

DONCASTER LIBRARY AND INFORMATION SERVICE	
3012202122023 7	
Askews	20-May-2004
	£10.75

Typeset by
Derek Doyle & Associates, Liverpool.
Printed and bound in Great Britain by
Antony Rowe Limited, Wiltshire

R. D.

CHAPTER ONE

Cresting the brow of the long, piñon-covered ridge, the small man on the tired bay stallion turned to survey his back trail.

What he saw there drew a hiss of displeasure from his thin lips as he urged his exhausted horse forward into the furnace heat and dust of the desert lands that began again at the foot of the treacherous slope which lay before his mount's hoofs. From the hatred that twisted his not unpleasant face, it seemed that whatever followed him was more to be feared than the arid, bitter land of south-western Sonora which lay before him.

Some miles behind, although he seemed much closer in the clear desert air, Jim Medway was urging a tired chestnut mare on to the first gentle upwelling which marked the beginning of the ridge his quarry had just left.

The man hunched deeper into the saddle, rolling a parched tongue against his teeth as he tried unsuccessfully to find enough moisture to clear even a portion of the dust that seemed to be caked solidly to his mouth and throat.

'If Hell's hotter'n this, Cocoa ol' gal,' he croaked, easing his lean, whipcord-tough body in the saddle, 'I guess we'd better mend our ways.'

He paused, signalling a stop gently through the reins, while he scanned the horizon, eyes aching against the white-hot glare. Experimentally, he raised one of the two-gallon canteens that hung from his saddle and gave it a gentle shake. The weight and soft sloshing seemed to reassure him, but still the Ranger shook his head and observed. 'We're gettin' kinda low, ol' gal. But that sissy Drago can't be no better off.' He scanned the horizon again, shielding his eyes ineffectually with a grimy palm, before reaching down to pat a dusty brown shoulder.

'And he ain't got a pony as good as mine for this kinda work,' he reassured himself grimly.

That thought may have passed briefly through Drago's mind some two hours later when the gallant bay stallion, unused to the heat and dust and flies of these desert lands, pulled up dead lame.

Drago wasted one full minute in vitriolic cursing before pulling a pistol and aiming it between the stallion's eyes. Only a single ounce of pressure stood between him and his suicidal mistake, when a soft, high-pitched whistle sounded nearby. Drago paused, lifting his Colt towards the sound as a low voice, a voice somehow infused with everything evil in human nature, said, 'I wouldn't be too quick to shoot that horse, *amigo*. You might have trouble finding another one.' Drago knew that voice and its educated accents and he shivered uncharacteristically at the sight of the black-dressed man with the two silver-mounted Colt Lightnings, who stepped noiselessly from the concealment of the surrounding rocks.

He somehow couldn't keep the quaver out of his voice as he nodded and said, 'D. . . Doc. Long time no—'

'Yeah, yeah,' the black-dressed one interrupted impatiently, 'Who's that following you?'

For a second, fear flooded Drago's mind as he sought for a lie that might help. Then, desperately, he whined. 'See, Doc, me and him had a little business. . . .'

Thirst and exhaustion always tend to make a man careless, especially approaching the end of something, and Medway would have needed to have looked no further for an excuse, if he had been the sort who ever bothered to try and excuse his mistakes.

As it was, one moment he was following a fresh plain trail that told him Drago was getting closer by the minute, when a rope twanged and he was jerked from the saddle, landing winded and barely conscious.

He woke abruptly to find himself gazing into a pair of baby-blue eyes that looked out of a pale, studious face of choir-boy innocence, given pause only by the sight of its owner's all-black cowboy gear and silver-mounted revolvers.

Over one thin, black-clad shoulder, Medway observed a desperately grinning Drago, but before he could speak the black-dressed figure said softly, 'Glad to see you here, Mr Medway. Drago tells me you and

7

he've done a little business in the past. Luckily for you, it might be the sort of business my principal would be interested in.'

Medway blinked. However the boy was dressed, his tone and accent were pure Boston.

Up close, Medway could see that his initial impression of the speaker's youth had been mistaken. Certainly, he wasn't old but there was a hardness around the mouth and a flaring, wicked light in the soft blue eyes that told its own story. To Medway, the whole screamed killer and his right hand, the one on the opposite side to his assailant's, was very close to its holstered Colt as he lurched to his feet.

Awkwardly, he shook his head, apparently to clear it, while he took in this new situation. By rights, he should be dead because, plainly, Drago's new friends were some way from being law-abiding citizens. And what possible motive could Drago have for keeping him alive? Mentally, Medway shrugged. All this could wait until later.

Carefully, he reached up and felt his head. Apparently satisfied with his inspection, Medway growled, 'Yeah, you could say that. Weren't nothin' illegal, though.'

The black-dressed man smiled. It wasn't a very nice smile.

'Opening safes sounds fairly illegal to me,' he said, as he jerked a thumb at his chest. 'I'm Doc, least that's what these range scourings call me. And if you ever lie to me again, Mr Medway, why, I believe I'll just naturally have to kill you.' There was no inflection, no emotion in the flat voice as he said this and Medway

8

felt an icy hand grip his spine. Whoever these people were, they made Drago's original bunch look like children.

They camped early that night and dusk was just falling as Medway collected a plate of food from one of the sullen young Mexicans who were tending the cook pot and sauntered across to where Drago was shovelling food into his mouth.

'Your manners'd make a hog puke,' Medway offered with a grimace. 'You look like you ain't ate fur a week.' Drago scraped up the last of his beans and glared hungrily at the plate in Medway's hands.

'It weren't quite that long,' he snarled, 'though you sure as hell ought to know, you was chasin' me hard enough!'

Medway twisted and the firelight threw red lights into his eyes as he said, 'You give me enough reason!' He paused, then sneered. 'Your li'l trick with the body outside Wayside didn't fool no one. I guessed it weren't you, but why in hell did you head this way? And why'd you tell that hydrophoby li'l skunk' – he jerked his chin to where Doc was walking towards the fire – 'that we was partners? He'd have killed me and saved you the trouble if you'd just told him the truth.'

For a tense moment, Drago glared back at the Ranger who had elected to become his Nemesis, then his eyes dropped and he said with a soft chuckle, 'I found what I was lookin' for. These here are friends o' mine and as for not tellin', why, I had reasons of—'

Drago was interrupted by the sound of a vicious slap echoing across the clearing.

Doc was standing over the shorter of the Mexican

cook boys, the mark of his blow plain as a badge on the boy's cheek.

'I told you,' he began slowly, 'I told you about serving up this greaser shit. From now on, for his sake, I hope your friend can cook American style.'

He shook his head slowly. 'See,' he continued softly, 'I don't think we want to keep a damn stupid, bean-eating greaser around who can't cook better than this.' He jerked the plate and the frijole beans flicked across the young man's shirt, causing him to jerk back with an expression of disgust. It was his last action in life, because before anyone realized what he intended, a Colt flowed into Doc's hand and a shot rang out. The prone boy screamed, clasping his hands to his stomach as a stream of crimson sluggishly flowed across his cheap, white trousers.

There was a second of stunned silence then, with an inarticulate scream of rage, the boy's companion threw himself towards the black-dressed killer of his friend. Doc's pistol flickered upwards and it seemed certain that the second boy must die as well, but, in a blur of motion, Medway was between them and his pistol was slamming with controlled force into the side of the boy's head, depositing him alive but unconscious, almost at Doc's feet.

'I don't know what you need me for,' Medway said slowly, 'but I don't like to cook, so I'm sayin' the kid lives. And unless you can do the job yourself, you better leather that piece. Less'n there's somewhere else you're figurin' on sticking it,' he finished shrewdly.

For a split second, the red light of murder flared in

Doc's eyes. Then he smiled and the blue eyes were mild as he said, 'Certainly, Medway, whatever you say. Can't be falling out with our new chums, can we?' He turned on his heel, glancing uninterestedly at his first victim.

'Just throw that' – he indicated the dying boy with a jerk of his chin – 'somewhere where it'll die quietly, will you?' he finished, as he headed for his bedroll.

Medway didn't relax until Doc had collected his blankets and headed off into the trees. Then he snapped at Drago. 'Give me a hand with these kids. And you needn't bother to explain about the story. If'n you'd told him you let someone like me follow you this far he'd've killed both of us, sure as hell.'

Drago shook his head.

'I don't need no help killin' you, Medway,' he sneered. 'And I ain't tendin' no greaser.' But Medway had heard the little whispering edge in the killer's voice.

'No, that ain' t quite true,' the Ranger replied, shaking his head. 'You ain't quite sure you can take me. Now me' – Medway was facing the bandit, his hand relaxed and ready by the worn black butt of his Colt – 'I know I can't take you, but I also know that there ain't enough of a difference for either of us to live on. Pull on me,' Medway finished gently, 'and we'll ride to hell together. And you ain't got the nerve for that!'

As the last word left his lips, Medway's hand slashed round, catching Drago a stinging slap on the cheek and knocking him sprawling in the dust. Through the haze of pain and humiliation, Drago heard the Ranger say, 'Go ahead, you won't never have a better excuse.'

Anger flared only to find good sense waiting for it. Keeping his hands in sight, Drago stumbled to his feet, mumbling through cracked lips, 'You'll keep.'

Medway nodded. 'Sure,' he offered, 'till then, get the kid's feet.'

There wasn't much left to do for the first of the boys. Every movement, every shift drew forth an agonized little squeak, it was hardly more, like a kitten in pain. Finally, Medway gave up, simply wrapping the boy in a couple of grimy blankets and leaving Drago with instructions to watch him.

Medway's victim was in better shape, sitting, head in hands, where the Ranger had dropped him. Squatting easily, Medway asked, 'You OK, son?' For a long second the boy looked at him, before abruptly vomiting.

When he'd finished, the boy wiped a hand across his mouth and said, 'You stopped me. Why? I am nothin' to you, jus' another greaser, good only for killing.'

Dispassionately, the Ranger examined the boy. 'All *gringos* ain't like him,' Medway stated flatly, jerking a thumb in Doc's direction, 'though I ain't saying killin' him mightn't be a bad idea. Only thing you did wrong was, you didn't pick your time; you let him pick it. That was a mistake. Don't make it again. If you can walk, we should see to your friend,' he finished.

'Carlito, Carlito.' The boy looked up at Medway from where he knelt by the blanket-clad figure of his friend. 'He must have medicine, a doctor! I must help him!'

Medway shook his head. 'You can't help him, kid,'

12

he said softly, 'but you got a choice: you can let him suffer all night, mebbe half of tomorrow or . . . you can show him real friendship.' The Ranger's voice was as soft as a woman's as he went on. 'It's a hard thing but . . . if'n I was him . . . I know what I'd want . . . and . . .' suddenly there was a Colt in his hand, butt forward – 'I know who I'd want to do it.' Carefully, he placed the weapon on the blanket and turned to walk away.

Swift though he was, he had barely taken two steps before there was the crack of a shot and hurrying footsteps. Turning, Medway took the proffered Colt and said gently, 'If you want a hand. . . .'

'No,' the boy snapped abruptly, then softened. 'No, thank you, *señor.*' He explained, 'Here we bury our own.'

Medway nodded, lips touched by a grim little smile, 'Where I come from, too.' he offered.

For a moment, the boy's face twisted, then he said abruptly, 'My name is Jose Negas, *señor,* and I – I – I. . . .'

Medway slapped him on the shoulder by way of interruption. 'Save it,' he said. 'I'll get you a shovel.'

CHAPTER TWO

Next morning, cold and breakfastless, Medway and his companions were in the saddle before dawn.

'We have to make the ranch today,' was Doc's only comment, when Drago complained about the early start, adding brightly, 'You don't have to come, you know.' Drago subsided as Doc gave a bark of laughter and spurred savagely ahead, leaving Medway with something to think about.

No one seemed particularly concerned about him or where he rode, so Medway drew rein next to a morose Drago.

'Don't seem so especially glad to see you,' he needled. Drago grunted, not deigning to be drawn. Medway tried again. 'Sure like old times,' he offered. 'Us headin' for a hideout you thought nobody knew about.'

Drago twisted as if stung, 'You don't want to make too much o' last time,' he snapped. 'You got lucky. This time you won't be up agin bar scourin's and border trash. And this hideout ain't a secret. It don't need to be. Georges is too clever for that.' Urgently,

14

he spurred his borrowed pony forward, leaving Medway to his memories.

What Drago had said was certainly partly true, Medway had been lucky the last time they'd met. He'd been sent to the little town of Wayside, to arrest this Lance Drago, who'd been heading a gang of outlaws responsible for terrorizing the surrounding country. It'd been personal, too, since Medway was sure that Drago had tortured to death his wife and baby son.

But Drago had been planning an enormous bank job, and when the specially imported Eastern safe blower was badly wounded trying to help Medway escape from Drago and his gang, the Ranger conned Drago into letting him take the man's place. Then, there'd been a lot of killing and Medway would have been the first to admit that, by surviving, he'd had more, much more, than his fair share of Texas luck.

At first, it seemed that Drago had been killed and Medway had achieved a measure of peace. But then he'd seen the report of the bandit's death and had known in a flash that it had been faked and how.

So he'd strapped on his worn Colts, collected his badge and turned Cocoa south.

Drago's trail had been plain, to anyone who knew where to look, and that was how Medway found himself, six months after the tunnel cave-in that nearly cost him his life, riding in company with a set of bandidos and killers who would tear him to pieces if they ever found out his real identity.

Early evening sun had barely begun to gild the mountain range which had dominated their journey for the last few hours, when Doc jerked his well-bred black gelding to a halt on a low rise in the rocky trail. As his men streamed past him, the black-dressed one turned in the saddle and beckoned Medway forward.

'Well, what do you think, my friend?' Doc demanded, with a theatrical wave of his hand.

Medway could only stare, stunned into silence. Before Cocoa's hoofs, the trail broadened and fell gently away into an enormous valley, covered in the green of succulents and grama grass. Everywhere was green, in stark contrast to the surrounding desert and, after a glance at the far end of the place, Medway understood the reason. From a crack high in the rock wall, a waterfall cascaded down over the red sandstone, forming a deep pool, some 200 yards in diameter. Nearby, on a gentle rise of land was a sprawling adobe ranch house, with verandas on the three sides visible from the trail, while a motley collection of other buildings were scattered behind, forming a rough square. On the nearest veranda a man sat facing the trail. Even at that distance, Medway could see he was well above average size. But the Ranger had also noted other things.

The house had been built so that one man with a rifle could deny access to the lake to anyone in the valley. Medway couldn't see it but he guessed there was a way down to the water which couldn't be overlooked by anyone with a rifle, even the guards. And there were plenty of those.

'And all this is yours?' Medway sneered.

'No,' Doc admitted. 'It belongs . . .' he paused, face twisting. 'I suppose you could call him my partner.

Come on,' the killer finished, 'he'll want to meet you.'

'I'm looking forward to it,' Medway lied. 'Oh and Doc,' he finished, as they moved forward, 'just so we're clear, I ain't your friend.'

Doc nodded as though encountering some deep human truth. 'I'm aware of it,' he said softly, glancing sideways. 'You may wish it was otherwise before you leave here. If you ever leave here.'

As the two men moved down the trail and from there on to the valley floor, Medway began to feel a grudging admiration for the unknown man in command, especially since he was well aware that he'd been covered by one or more of the men in the rocks since he'd entered the valley. More importantly, they looked alert and handled their weapons with all the familiarity of long practice, without any of the greaser tendency to get together for conversation and siesta. Whoever was responsible for that would need watching.

Doc jerked his gelding to a halt in front of the veranda, screening the Ranger from any view of the man seated there. Medway pulled Cocoa back, glancing across at the giant figure as Doc sneered, 'I found Drago on the trail. This was following him. Drago says he may be useful, though I've yet to be convinced.' But Medway wasn't listening. His attention was riveted on the figure on the porch.

Propped on the bar which ran across the veranda at waist height were a pair of boots, wearing the silver-mounted spurs with rowels of fifty-dollar gold pieces which had haunted so many of Medway's dreams. Those spurs, and the giant of a man who wore them, had been the only thing he could remember about that day, now so long ago, when his family had been murdered. That and Lucy screaming.

His eyes moved away from the boots to their owner. Even sitting down he was clearly enormous, but when he spoke, his voice was soft, almost womanish.

'So. Always it is good to see ol' frens, *amigo*. Where is he, Drago, the so leetle snake?'

'Howdy, Georges,' Drago offered, pulling up behind and to the left of Medway. 'L – long time, no see.' Medway clearly heard the fear in the little killer's voice and wondered. The big man ignored him.

'I am Georges Medina,' he began elaborately, addressing Medway. 'Owner and *alcalde* of this, how you say, this leetle community. Come inside. And leave the guns on your saddle, *por favor*.'

Despite the light tone, it was plainly an order and equally certain, from the way Medina's hand dropped to his belt and the glitter in Doc's eyes, if Medway didn't obey, he'd be shot down without mercy.

Carefully, keeping every movement slow and easy, Medway unbuckled his twin holsters and hooked the belt carefully on to the saddle horn. Drago had already complied and was now standing awkwardly on the dusty bottom step, clearly unsure what he should do next. Even as Medway eased himself out of the saddle, still uncomfortably aware of Doc's icy stare, Drago blurted, 'Christ, Georges, what's the hell d'you think you're doin'? I ride all this way out here so we can join up like before. Hell, I even brung you a safe blower, 'cause I figure he'll mebbe come in useful, and you treat me like I got the itch! What's the big idea?'

For all the attention Medina paid him, Drago might have been some insect buzzing at him from the dust. Without looking in Drago's direction, the Mexican said, 'OK, le's all have a leetle drink. Come on.' He gestured with a hand that looked to Medway about the size of a side of bacon and waddled into the house.

Wonderingly, Medway followed, to find himself in a large, airy, lime-washed room the central feature of which was an enormous, ornate, flat-topped desk, littered with papers. Medina seated himself awkwardly behind the desk, waving everyone to chairs while he swivelled around and appeared to be staring intently out of the window. One minute dragged by endlessly and still he stared, with the others unwilling or unable to break the silence. Then abruptly, Medina jerked his head towards Drago and snapped, 'Why did you come here, *amigo?*'

Drago shrugged abruptly. 'W-we're partners—' he began, in the voice of a man badly scared.

Medina interrupted with a bark of laughter. 'We *were* partners,' he corrected. 'Your share was to be the money from the Wayside bank. You mebbe got that in your pockets . . . *amigo?*' Doc gave a grunt which might have been amusement but Medina ignored him.

'You understood the deal,' Medina went on gently. 'You get the money, then I get the men an' the guns. So simple. But you no get the money – and this is the part that hurts me – I must find this out from another.' He paused and his voice was soft and icy as he said, 'Why shouldn't I kill you, now?' His hand fluttered and there was a pistol pointing at the centre of Drago's forehead as Medina whispered into the sudden stillness. 'Eh, *amigo*, why not?'

Sweat broke out in an icy dew on Drago's forehead as he tried to force words past the fear in his throat. The pistol barrel was growing, a great dark tunnel, with eternity at the end of it, when a cloud of tobacco smoke swept between the two men and a cold, Texas voice said, ' 'Cause you can't have too many Americanos sidin' you if you gotta work north of the Rio Bravo.'

The pistol barrel never wavered, but there was curiosity in Medina's voice as he asked softly, 'An' who say we go north of el Rio Bravo, *señors?*'

Medway sighed, 'You bin dealing with stupid bastards too long, Georges,' he began easily. 'There ain't nothin' in this flea-bitten country worth a hundred dollars, not since Juarez hung all the Frenchies, let alone the sort o' money you're thinkin' o' layin' out. No' – he settled back complacently – 'you're goin' north and, what's more, you need that li'l pissant and you know it.'

'I do?' Medina returned, holstering his weapon with a flourish and leaning back. 'What make you so verra sure, *Señor?*'

'Medway,' Medway offered. 'Jim Medway. And I'm sure 'cause if you didn't need him, he'd never have got here alive. Tell you something else for free too,' he continued, 'you figure you need me, and afore you ask, I know for the same reason,' he finished.

For a moment, the big man glared at Medway across the desk, then he threw back his head and peals of high-pitched laughter rang across the ceiling.

Abruptly, Medina regained control and, still wiping

his eyes, said, 'Lucky you bring this one along, my friend,' he offered, addressing Drago. 'Lucky for us, maybe lucky for him, but especially . . . verra lucky for you, *amigo*.' And the threat suddenly lay stark and clear in the large room. Medway grimaced. Clearly, this was a reprieve, nothing more.

The cool evening air with its scent of pine felt good as Medway left the hacienda and went in search of a place for his horse. He walked silently towards the complex of barns and horse corrals, checking shadows, hand brushing gun butt. He had a lot to think about but it was better to leave it until later. People got murdered down Mexico way for much less than a good horse and two Colts.

Suddenly, a whisper of noise drifted out of the darkness and a Colt leapt, almost of its own accord into Medway's hand.

'Step into the light and make it pronto, you greaser bastard,' Medway snapped, suddenly aware of moonlight behind him and the uncomfortable proximity of an adobe fenced horse corral.

From a point apparently next to his left shoulder a voice Medway knew well said, 'Now, Jim boy, be that any way to talk to old friends?'

CHAPTER THREE

'So have you two done anything 'cept get drunk and chase gals since Cap Palmiter sent you that telegram? And what made you come here?' Medway demanded, as he gently brushed alkali dust from Cocoa's chestnut hide.

'First off, nope,' admitted the taller and thinner of the pair with an unabashed grin. 'We ain't bin doin' nothin' but ride around admirin' the scenery. An' when your boss said you was still trailin' Drago, we knew you'd end up here, 'cause Drago and Medina bin doin' business for years. This is where we first heard about the Wayside job,' he finished seriously.

Medway studied the other for a moment, then said mildly, 'That's interesting.' Turning to the second of the pair, he asked, 'So how's it look, Slim?'

The little fat man seated on a nearby barrel hitched the broad belt with its twin holsters and scowled.

'It looks legal, more or less, is how it looks,' he admitted. 'Only thing I could say was a li'l out of line, he's got mebbe three times as many *vaqueros* as he needs.' His tall friend shook his head and the little man snapped, 'If'n you got somethin' to say, Shorty, you damn stringbean, spit it out and stop shakin' that thing you keep your hat on!'

The tall one raised his eyes to heaven and said slowly, 'See, ol' Slim's bein' kinda . . . misleadin' there, Jim,' he offered easily. 'Medina's got about the right number o' cowhands fer the work. What he didn't say was there are about twice as many more just loafin' around, who wouldn't know one end of a cow from the other even if you painted 'em a picture. Howsomever,' he continued, ignoring his irate friend, 'I'm guessing they're right smart when it comes to guns and knives and such.'

'*Pistoleros*, Shorty?' Medway asked. '*Americanos del Norte?*'

Slim interrupted briskly, 'He's right, for a wonder,' he snapped, glaring at his complacent partner, who suddenly stiffened and jerked his head towards the outer door. 'I guess it had to happen sometime, laws o' chance bein' what they are. He's got a few Americanos,' he continued, in a whisper, quickly signalling his tall friend into a nearby vacant stall. 'None of them much good except that black-dressed bastard and he's very good.'

'There's only one, Jim, comin' this way. Shorty, get. . . .' the little man urged in a whisper, before he saw the tall shadow by the door with the glint of moonlight in its fist.

When Medway looked back, he was alone, except for the shadows, and the door of the barn was swinging open. It was Doc.

'See you found it,' he began without preamble.

23

'Boss wants to see you tomorrow morning. It's business, so don't go to any trouble,' he sneered, glancing over the other's worn range clothes.

Medway nodded. 'I won't,' he answered, before sniffing hard and asking mildly, 'Say, you ain't brought a skunk in here with you, have you, Doc?' He sniffed again and said, 'Nope, that ain't sku— Hell, Doc I believe it's you! What you bin dousin' yourself in, sheep dip?'

Doc, who paid ninety dollars a bottle for the bay rum concoction he used on his hair, coloured visibly, and said with an effort at control, 'Tomorrow, after breakfast,' and turned on his heel.

'Now, you be careful, Doc,' Medway called solicitously after him. 'You never know what you're gonna run into after dark, especially smellin' like that. I hear tell there's a lot o' vermin around here.'

Doc paused in the doorway, looking back. 'I'm wearing an answer to any vermin problem,' he snapped, tapping one of the pearl-butted Colt Lightnings.

Medway had been working on Cocoa for some minutes, when he heard a gentle rubbing from the front wall of the stable. It was just the sort of sound a man would dismiss and Medway made a long stroke down his pony's already gleaming flank, before saying, 'So is there anything else about this place that don't run true?'

Shorty slipped noiselessly through the door as Slim squirmed himself to comfort on his barrel seat and said, 'There was somethin'. Ain't no peons around the place.'

'Cattle ranch,' Medway shrugged. 'Don't need farmers.'

'Sure,' Shorty agreed, without taking his eyes from the moonlight-shadowed yard beyond the door, ' 'ceptin' about once, twice a month, a wagonload of 'em turn up, fill five mebbe six supply wagons and head off. Got a couple o' them imitation *pistoleros* guardin' 'em. No one's allowed to have nothin' to do with 'em. Fella went to the corral last week 'cause Doc claimed he rode out too close after the wagons.'

Medway looked across at the tall man. 'Went to the corral?' he demanded. 'Why, did that black-dressed *pedalo* make 'im leave?'

Slim shook his head. 'No,' he said quietly. 'Ol' Pedro went feet first. An' he was a tough *hombre*. Couldn't want a better, gun or knife. So don't you sell your friend in black short.'

'Why?' Medway demanded.

' 'Cause ol' Pedro had a knife and Doc killed him with his bare hands,' came the quiet answer.

Sun-up found Cocoa fed and watered and Medway returning to the tiny cantina where he had spent a comfortless night. Possibilities were turning themselves over in his mind, with Medina and his involvement in Lucy's death well to the fore, when his attention was jerked back to the present by a familiar sound, the slap of leather and the click of a pistol cocking at the end of it.

Nearby was a narrow gap between two buildings and it was from here that the sound seemed to be coming. Silent as a cougar, Medway edged across the sand and inched his face past the corner of sun-blasted adobe.

Negas, the boy whom Medway had saved, was crouched with his back to the Ranger, hand hovering above a dilapidated holster from which protruded an ancient revolver. As Medway watched, the hand dropped swiftly, jerking the revolver free, the thumb easing back the hammer. Smoothly, the weapon rose level and the hammer snapped down on the bare nipple of the old percussion weapon.

With a grunt of contempt, the boy thrust the old weapon away and prepared to try again, only to freeze motionless as Medway said softy, 'Your holster's too high and you better get somethin' that'll shoot better'n that ol' relic if you're goin' after Doc.' He advanced towards the boy and held out his hand.

'Let me just see that shootin'-iron, *amigo*.' Medway knocked out the pin and squinted up the barrel, then he grunted and said, 'Lucky for you, you ain't never tried to fire this. Barrel's so full o' rust she'd just plumb blow your hand clean off if'n you did.' For a moment, he studied the crestfallen young man staring back at him with a set mouth and hard angry eyes. Then he nodded and put out an arm.

'First,' the Ranger began, 'we gotta find you a safer place to practice. Then, I'll show how to do it right.' He nodded, speaking half to himself. 'Practice is sure necessary if'n you want to be good with anything. But you got to be practicin' the right way. And we better see about a decent pistol, too.'

Wonderingly, the boy allowed himself to be led through the brush only to suddenly jerk back and demand, 'Why you do this?'

Medway looked him over carefully. 'I need some information,' he answered, with a hard smile. 'Also . . . you might call it . . . insurance.'

The sun was well over the neighbouring mountain peaks when Medway finally stamped through the door of Medina's office, where Doc and the Mexican were deep in conversation and, slumping into a chair, began unconcernedly to construct a smoke.

'You're late!' the rancher snapped from the depths of an over-stuffed leather armchair, which occupied the opposite side of the ornate desk. Medway shrugged, concentrating on his smoke.

'Ol' Skunk Breath . . . I mean Doc,' he began, before apparently correcting himself, 'said it was just business and not to hurry. He also said not to dress up, though I see you ain't taken his advice. Sure must be a few pimps in Dallas wondering what they gonna wear tonight.' Medina appeared not to hear, although his gold and silver-decorated hidalgo costume would have passed for the height of bad taste anywhere.

'Since you are here now,' the Mexican began, 'perhaps you would like to hear a leetle proposition.' He paused, waiting for a response. When none was forthcoming, he went on angrily, 'Soon, like you guess, we gonna be riding north. There will be much gold, women, easy pickin' for all. And maybe one or two so verra little safes to open. That is where you come in. But first,' Medina went on, before Medway could speak, 'you gotta pass a leetle test.'

'Test!' Medway snorted with laughter. 'Now here's

me thinkin' I've run up agin this gang o' real dangerous *hombres* but no . . . I'm wrong, it's a goddamn kids' schoolroom. What sort of test is it?' he demanded. 'You want me to mebbe spell "Stick your job up your—" '

'Now, that's enough, friend,' Doc snapped, moving out from behind Medina's chair. 'You can't expect us to cut you in on something as sweet as this is going to be without making sure you can do what's required.'

'How sweet?' Medway demanded, hoping for something solid.

'Sweet enough, gringo,' flashed Medina, rising and crossing the floor. 'But before you find out any more, I want you to prove you are who you say you are.'

'Drago vouched for me,' Medway said quietly, shifting to bring a Colt under his hand.

'Sure,' Medina admitted, 'Or you be dead right now. But mebbe he lie . . . so now you show me: you open this,' he finished, pulling an ornate cloth from a large square safe standing against the wall.

Medway glared despairingly at the green and gold monster as Medina went on, 'Drago, he say you can open this wid just your fingers and tools. No need dynamite. Tha's good, 'cause we ain't got none. You show me . . . *now.*'

The last word dropped into the sudden stillness like a stone. Medway rose from his chair and, moving between the two men, knelt to examine the safe. For several long seconds, he made a pretence of sounding the door and checking the hinges, mind whirling for a way out.

It was certainly a big safe, but even Medway could see it was of a very ancient vintage. There was no combination lock, the door being secured by a single key. Slowly, he leaned back and straightened to his feet, the germ of an idea beginning to form. It was a long shot, but, as Medway freely admitted to himself, he was all out of safe options.

Turning to Medina, the Ranger said, 'This is a piece of junk. A kid with a hair pin could open it. By the way, who's got the key?'

Before Medina could answer, Doc broke in, 'I do and, before you ask, no, I couldn't lend it to you!' he sneered.

Medway shrugged and spread his hands. 'I wasn't . . . Christ, how did that get in here?'

If it wasn't the oldest trick in the book, it was close and Doc, to his credit, only half fell for it. His eyes flickered away, following Medway's glance and in the instant allowed him, the Ranger smashed the hard, leather-lined tip of his Texas boot into the soft tissue just below the killer's knee. Doc's mouth opened in a soundless scream, abruptly terminated as Medway's iron fist smashed into the side of his jaw, dropping him like a stone. Before the Mexican had even thought about moving, he was looking into the yawning bore of Medway's Colt. Medina's hands went ceilingward with embarrassing swiftness and Medway nodded, speaking almost to himself.

'Figure anyone hires it done ain't got the nerve to use a gun theirselves.'

Medina coloured swiftly. 'You lie,' he screamed. 'Give me a fair chance and I will kill you, gringo.'

Swifter than sight, Medway's gun leapt back into the holster. He bent, jerked Doc's pistol free and his hand flicked like a snake striking. Medina had no time to dodge and the heavy weapon caught him full in the face, mashing lips and nose to jam. Heedless of his danger or the job, heedless of everything but his aching desire to kill, Medway leapt the intervening space and grasping Medina's carefully oiled hair, wrenched the bandit upright. His Colt's hammer eared back and he shoved the worn barrel between the bandit's blood-slobbering lips.

Medway's finger was tightening on the trigger, steeling himself to kill in cold blood, when a sound, coming from behind him, penetrated the red mist filling his mind. Slowly his vision cleared and he became aware that someone, somewhere was softly clapping, and a voice said, 'That was very entertaining. But the question still remains: just how do you intend to open that safe?'

CHAPTER FOUR

Slowly, Medway twisted his head to find himself under the scrutiny of three newcomers, who had clearly just come through a door, previously concealed by a hanging, which now stood half open.

There was a girl, tall, dark-haired and voluptuous, dressed in boots and simple riding outfit, alongside a giant Mexican, both standing behind the third figure, who was seated in an iron-framed chair mounted on little wheels. Despite his obvious disability, Medway's eyes flicked back to this one after surveying the group. Mentally, he nodded.

This had to be the one, the driving force the whole set up revolved around. The seated figure spoke again.

'If you have no pressing desire to kill Señor Medina, perhaps you would put him down. I find greasers personally distasteful, Mr Morgan, but this one has his uses. And I would ask again, how do you plan to get into that safe?'

Without warning, Medway flipped his gun out of the Mexican's mouth and abruptly smashed the barrel across the bridge of Medina's nose. His victim subsided, screaming, and pushing him to one side with

31

the toe of his boot, Medway stepped easily across and began methodically to search the pockets of a groaning Doc until he fished out a small bunch of keys.

Carelessly, he tossed them into the seated man's lap before saying, 'Even brainless scum like this oughta know I can't open a safe without tools.' He grinned, before adding ingratiatingly, ' Pros like us'll allus take the easy way, anyhow.'

The other nodded, smiling slightly and said reasonably, 'And you couldn't have perhaps ... ah ... explained that to them in a less emphatic fashion?'

'They was pushing,' Medway snapped aggressively, 'an' I don't like to be pushed. And while we're on the subject, who the hell are you ... and them?' he demanded, gesturing absently with a Colt-filled hand.

'Wilson, Clarence Wilson,' the other acknowledged. 'These are my associates, Hernandez and his sister, Marcia,' he added, indicating the man and girl in turn. 'It was my son, Eustace, whose knee you almost broke. But I don't think I'll hold it against you. Although, of course,' he finished, with a soft, cultured laugh, 'he might.'

By this time, Doc was stirring and, as he pushed himself up shakily from the floor, Wilson jerked his chair forward, grabbed up a vicious-looking riding crop that had been hidden in his lap and slashed the black-dressed man across the face. Doc jerked back, the weal on his cheek dripping blood as Wilson spat, 'Another failure! There were two of you and you let him take you!'

Doc glared over his father's shoulder at a grinning Medway, who had holstered his weapon and was enjoying the other's discomfiture.

'He tricked me,' Doc mumbled past a swelling cheek and was barely able to jerk back in time to avoid a second blow.

'Excuses are for weaklings!' the old man screamed. For a moment, Wilson was still, fists clenching and unclenching, then he hissed, 'Luckily, you still have some uses. Degas goes to the corral this morning. Get out and prepare. And . . . don't fail!'

Doc's eyes glinted, with hatred and something else, then he nodded.

Wilson swung his head back towards Medway as his son left the room, followed by a staggering Medina.

'We have a rather unique way of maintaining discipline amongst our people here,' he offered smoothly. 'Perhaps you would be interested to observe the process?'

Gone was all trace of anger and the Ranger was thoughtful as he answered, 'Sure.'

Warily, hands close to the weapons at his side, Medway followed Hernandez out into the morning glare. Side by side, they trudged towards an area of the ranch that Medway had not seen before. Up ahead, a hatless Doc was walking fast in the same direction.

Medway hazarded a question. 'The big boss, he doesn't watch his son?'

Without moving his head, Hernandez laughed and said, 'No, mebbe you notice, they don' like each other much.'

Medway nodded and risked another question, 'Any reason for that?'

For a moment, Hernandez's glance flicked across

the other and Medway held his breath. But the cold brown eyes held no trace of suspicion as the big man rumbled, 'No secret, I guess, Old Señor Wilson, he love the boy's mother verra much. They are, how the gringo say, sweettooths?'

'Sweethearts,' Medway corrected tightly.

'Ah, *si, estas bien.* Sweethearts.' Hernandez went on, 'But the Missus Wilson, she is not strong. She die birthin' th' boy and the old one, he never forgive his son.'

Medway nodded and said, 'And you and your sister, you work for him long?'

This time the shutters dropped and suspicion flared as Hernandez snapped, 'Long enough. You a verra nosy *hombre*, Texas.'

Medway gave a grin he was far from feeling and said easily, 'Just curious about the set up.' Adding, meaningfully, 'Wouldn't want there to be no mistakes.'

Hernandez's mouth spread in a grimace, showing the stumps of blackened teeth.

'Oh there won't be no mistakes, Texas. Not unless you make 'em.'

Approaching the corral, Hernandez briefly examined the bars and then, shouldering two men aside, said, 'Here, this is where we get the best view.'

Noting the man's flaring nostrils and quickened breathing, Medway wondered what might lay in wait for him.

He wasn't left in doubt long. He had barely time to notice Slim and Shorty take position a little way from him, when Doc ducked under the middle bar of the corral and walked slowly to the centre. He raised a hand and the bedlam of shouting, catcalls and betting died as though cut off with an axe.

'There is a man amongst us,' Doc began without preamble, 'who has offended against the rules of the Brotherhood!' The noise swelled in volume, only to subside again as Doc held up an imperious hand and said, 'He has damaged one of the girls in the establishment of Señor Sanchez!' This time the roar was louder and Medway looked a question at Hernandez. The giant shrugged.

'He broke her jaw when she wouldn't. . .' The rest of the sentence was an obscene sucking sound and Medway nodded, grimacing, as he turned back to the figure in the centre of the corral. Doc's audience had quietened now and the black-dressed figure continued theatrically.

'For this crime, there is one penalty: death.' The roar of approval which greeted this speech coincided with the appearance of two men, holding a third, who struggled and whimpered. This one, obviously the intended victim, would plainly have begged for mercy but was prevented by a vicious wooden gag which had been twisted so hard into the victim's mouth that blood had dribbled out and dried on his chin.

At a signal from Doc, the man was pitched face forward to the dust of the corral, one of his guards stooping swiftly and slashing the ropes that bound his wrists before wrenching the gag from his mouth.

Slowly, the man raised his face, transfixed with fear at the apparently innocuous sight of Doc slowly pulling on a pair of thick, black leather gloves. That done, the Easterner jerked his chin and one of the guards tossed a long, narrow-bladed knife into the dust in front of the prisoner, while the killer himself reached into the back strap of his Levis and drew out a vicious-looking quirt, lovingly running his fingers through the thongs as he approached his victim.

Apparently, Degas knew better than to wait, and Doc's quirt cut only thin air as the little man snatched up the blade and leapt desperately backwards. Seeing Doc's inexorable advance, the Mexican whined, 'Doc, is me, Degas. *Amigo*, you ain't gonna kill me over some two-bit whore. . . .' That was as far as he got because Doc covered the remaining distance between them in a single jump and the quirt slashed sideways. There was a roar of animal approval from the crowd and Medway's breakfast nearly reappeared because the quirt had struck full upon the man's left eyeball, smashing it like an egg.

But Degas, under the whining, was tough and game. He ducked the backhand slash of Doc's unencumbered left and rolled away, pawing desperately at his good eye to clear it, the knife forgotten in his hand.

Almost daintily, Doc moved in, following the quirt. But Degas still had a trick or two. As Doc prepared to leap again, Degas dropped and the knife flickered upwards, driving in towards Doc's groin. But, almost magically, the black-dressed killer wasn't there.

Degas blundered past and Doc smashed a backhand blow into his face, knocking him screaming into the dust, only feet from where Medway stood.

Slowly, the little man raised up on to his elbows and Medway glared in horror at the blood-oozing wreck that was Degas' left cheek. Somehow Doc's blow had cut to the bone and Medway could even see the white tendon slivers moving as Degas' face worked, trying somehow to relieve the unspeakable agony.

Desperately, the Mexican managed to force himself upright and, still clutching the knife, turned to face his tormentor. Slowly, drawing out his pleasure, Doc approached his tottering victim. Almost as if by accident, he appeared to move within knife range and Degas suddenly lunged, only to feel the slash of the quirt as it opened his other cheek. Staggering, the little man tried to turn, driving the knife at his opponent, only to have Doc slip away and send him sprawling. This time there was no escape.

Too deep in shock to move, Degas lay helpless as Doc slipped a boot under his chest and turned him over. For a moment, Doc stood with both arms raised as the crowd enthusiastically applauded, then he lunged and the quirt slashed across Degas' chest, cutting through to the bone.

Again and again Doc struck, until his left arm was bloody to the elbow and the quirt was sodden and thick with crimson slime.

Finally, he stood back and Medway sickened as he heard the satisfaction in the killer's voice, the sense of appetite satisfied, as he said, 'Hang that somewhere everyone can see it.' Without another word, he ducked through the bars of the corral and walked rapidly back towards the little collection of buildings that surrounded the main house.

'One o' them girls of Sanchez gonna get worked over real good now,' Hernandez laughed, and Medway looked his question. The big man shrugged.

'Everyone knows the Doc, he can only. . . .' –

Hernandez spat an obscure Mexican phrase, accompanied by an incredibly obscene gesture – 'after a killing.' Medway nodded resignedly, fighting with his stomach. Somehow, it would have been out of character if Doc hadn't been that way.

Sickened by what he had seen, Medway headed for the tiny cantina. Turning a corner, he was suddenly aware of a figure moving at him from one side. A swift turn was all that saved him as a viciously used gun butt smashed a glancing blow into the side of his head.

Desperate and half stunned, he tried to roll away, intent only on defending himself, when, like siren song through a veil of mist, he heard a woman's voice.

'For Chris'sake, what you do, you goddamn fool?' There was a mumbled reply, too low for Medway to hear, then a vicious laugh.

'Revenge!' said the same voice. 'We're playin' for millions an' you gonna tip our hand 'cause this one done you wrong? *Ay caramba...*' She lapsed into Spanish and shock bit into Medway as he heard the hate-filled voice of Lance Drago.

'He's dangerous,' Drago rasped. 'I made the mistake of thinkin' I could use him once before but—'

'That time you din' have me along,' the girl interrupted. 'You had a good plan last time. Trouble was, you underestimate the gringo. This time that ain't gonna happen because this time....' The voices faded as Medway desperately tried to hang on to consciousness but it was no use. A black pit loomed before him and, almost gratefully, he dived into it.

CHAPTER FIVE

It was the taste of whiskey on his tongue and the vague scent of horse that brought Medway staggering back through the gates of consciousness.

He opened his eyes to find his head pillowed on the narrow, linen-clad knee of Jose Negas and the youth whistled with relief when he found Medway had returned to the land of the living.

'*Madre de Dios, amigo*,' he gasped, 'I thought you was killed that time!'

Medway shook this head, then wished he hadn't. Clutching his temple, the Ranger said evenly, 'It was only a hard head and blind luck that made the difference.'

Negas nodded sympathetically. 'Accidents, they happen in this town.' He shrugged meaningfully, 'Mebbe you should go some place else . . . to live.'

Medway had begun to have thoughts along those lines himself when Doc called for him the next morning.

'My father requests the presence of your esteemed company,' Doc began. 'That is,' he added, with a sneer, as he noticed Medway's bedraggled appearance, 'if you can drag yourself away from the whiskey bottle for that long.'

A reply seemed like too much effort, so Medway gingerly clapped his hat over the swollen lump on his skull and followed Doc out, instinctively loosening his Colts in their greasy, tied-down holsters. Noticing the precaution, Doc was moved to sneer, 'They won't help you, if he wants you dead.' Adding bitterly, 'Believe me, I know.'

Wilson was waiting for Medway in a small office just off of the main room of the sprawling house. It was simply furnished with several rows of bookshelves against the walls, and a plain desk and chair placed near the window.

Wilson himself was sitting behind the desk busily writing, when the Ranger sauntered in. He waved his visitor to a chair and Medway sank into it easily, giving the arms a twitch to bring them out of line with the man opposite. Then he stiffened, because pull as he might, the chair remained immovable.

Carefully, Medway began a swift examination of the room and its owner. No one fixed a chair to the floor without having a good reason and Medway's cold glance swiftly checked the panels and bookshelves facing him. There was nothing and he was searching desperately for some innocent excuse which would allow him to examine the wall behind him when his glance fell on Clarence Wilson's wheelchair.

Its arms were of thick, padded red velvet, with what looked like a small, wide bar underneath. The padded portion of the arm projected well in front of this bar, throwing its front into deep shadow, but, as Medway examined it, he could make out what looked like a wide tube, about the size of a Colt's muzzle, embedded in the timber. He grinned faintly. Clearly Mr Wilson was a man who covered all bets. Medway squirmed deeper into his chair and prepared to enjoy himself.

Before long, Wilson drew a neat line under his penmanship and placed it carefully on top of a small pile of similar looking documents at his elbow. Leaning back, he removed his glasses and appeared to be examining Medway, who was entertaining himself by blowing smoke rings at the ceiling. Neither man spoke and it was Wilson who cracked first.

'You seem to be a man who knows what he wants, Mr Medway,' Wilson snapped. Medway shrugged, without removing his attention from the ceiling.

'I can use men like that and for the right man, the rewards could be . . . shall we say . . . substantial.'

Medway allowed his eyes to slide towards the desk as he said, 'That over-stuffed greaser dog o' yourn said something like that yesterday, afore he started playing kid's games. So, question is, how much is substantial?'

Wilson leaned back, steepling his hands and said pompously, 'It wouldn't be going too far to say that we were playing for the wealth of the entire south-western United States.'

Controlling his laughter with difficulty, Medway said. 'Well, that's certainly . . . substantial.'

Wilson must have sensed his amusement because he snapped, 'It's no joke, believe me. There is, in Mexico City, a growing body of rich, radical intellectuals who believe that the time has come for Mexico to reclaim the lands stolen from it centuries ago, by the United States. I represent those men, and together with certain individuals I have recruited' – he paused, sweeping a hand towards the door – 'a small number of whom you see around me, we intend to occupy those lands of South Texas, Arizona and New Mexico which were stolen from the brave ancestors of these men and proclaim the Republic of New Texas!' He raised a hand, beckoning, and Doc, Medina, Drago and the woman Marcia filed into the room and took their places behind Wilson's chair, all that is, except Drago, who was content to lounge by the open door, in front and to Medway's left.

Easily, Medway shifted, moving both feet flat on the floor and bringing his hand to rest on the butt of his off side Colt. Slowly, like a man deep in thought, he said, 'And just how much is . . . substantial . . . in hard cash?'

Wilson shrugged. 'To begin with, like the rest of us, my friend, your share will be the gratitude of the Tejas Republic,' he said smoothly.

'And pickings,' Doc added.

'And you want me to join you for the glory and pickings,' Medway snapped, feigning anger. 'I ain't about to work for charity,' he stated flatly. 'An' I never seen a revolution yet as turned a dollar for anyone at the end where the bullets was flyin'. My fee for this sort of work is fifty bucks a day, in gold, up front. Think about it, 'cause I'll be across the border in Paesar Querte. At least for a while.' Suddenly, there was a gun in his hand, menacing Drago, while Medway now occupied

42

the arm of the chair. 'There's too many accidents happenin' to people in this dump to suit me.'

Without taking his eye from Drago, Medway said softly, 'Think about it, Wilson. I'd like to work with you, we're the same sort. But I ain't comin' in for either peanuts or promises.' Brusquely, the Colt motioned a fuming Drago away from the door.

Framed in the exit, the Ranger added, 'And I can't see what the hell a revolution needs with a safe blower, anyhow.'

Medway had been gone for only a brief while when the girl said evenly, 'Perhaps you should have told him the truth.'

Wilson glanced up and smiled slightly. 'No.' He shook his head. 'He just needs a little persuasion.' He turned back to the page in front of him and so failed to see the look of malevolent hatred his son threw his way.

Without speaking, Doc left the house, beckoning as he did so to a scar-faced Mexican, who immediately left his three companions to join him. For some moments, Doc spoke softly, then the scar-faced one collected his companions and headed for the largest of the horse corrals. Doc nodded. At least now, there would be one less fly in the ointment.

Medway and Cocoa had been on the trail to the border long enough for the sunset to begin to gild the faraway peaks a gentle gold when the back of the Ranger's neck began to itch. Obedient to the signal, Medway drew the little pony into a convenient thicket beside the trail and, leaving her reins trailing, he swarmed into the lower branches of a nearby cotton-wood.

Carefully, he scanned his back-trail and, against the last rays of the sun, was rewarded by the sight of four ponies, pushing hard along it.

'Too fast and sure to be bandits followin' on the off chance,' he told himself, as he collected Cocoa and swung aboard. 'So we'll just arrange a li'l surprise for 'em.' Briefly, he scanned his surroundings, then set off towards what looked like a promising draw.

'Guess it's about time we bedded down for the night, Cocoa, ol' gal,' he informed the little mare.

'Huh, like candy from a baby,' Cruzes informed his bosom friend Diego, as they examined the tracks which led into the little canyon where Medway had elected to spend the night. Sanchez, the scar-faced leader, grunted and swung down.

'Domingo,' he said, addressing the fourth member of the group, who was scarcely more than a boy, 'you watch the horses.'

'We'll wait until it is good an' dark,' he began, indicating the other two. 'Then, go in the front door. Diego, you take care of the pony and we'll handle the rest.' He shrugged and a wicked smile marred his features. 'The gringo, he will sleep verra sound after this.'

Moonlight dappled the little clearing at the end of the draw, throwing the blanket-wrapped shape by the fire into sharp relief. Sanchez paused, searching anxiously, before hearing the reassuring whiffle of a pony from the shadow of a stunted pine tree. A hand signal sent Diego about his work and together the remaining two crept towards the fire. They were fifty yards from the blanket-wrapped shape, between the fire and the pine tree, when Sanchez threw his rifle to his shoulder and fired. Cruzes swiftly followed suit, both men riddling the Ranger's body, their noise masking the small but significant sounds coming from Cocoa's bed ground.

Savagely, Sanchez jerked up his weapon and advanced towards the body. Carefully slanting his gun towards the dead man he kicked aside the hat and the blanket to find himself staring at a neatly tied pile of brushwood.

Before Sanchez could react, a voice snapped from the darkness. 'Put up your hands, you're under arrest.' Sanchez and his companions put up their hands all right, but when they put them up, they were full of guns.

Slamming two rapid shots into the surrounding darkness, Sanchez sprinted towards the cover of a nearby rock pile. Cruzes, working his gun like a madman, was not so fortunate. A Winchester cracked once and he was thrown backwards, hit in the chest and dying.

Medway's second shot tore through the fat part of Sanchez' calf as the big man fell headlong behind his cover. Ignoring the pain, Sanchez wormed forward, rifle pointing towards the shadow under the pine from where he was sure the shots had come. A long minute passed without further shooting until, irritated beyond endurance by the silence and creeping pain in his leg, he slammed two shots in the direction of his tormentor. They whined away into the darkness and, as Sanchez strained his eyes towards the tree, there was a dry click behind him and Medway's voice was saying, 'With cartridges so expensive and hard to get, you shouldn't go wastin' them thataway.'

Without being told, Sanchez dropped his rifle and threw up both hands. He forced a look of surprise on to his unhandsome face before twisting around.

'*Señor*,' he began, innocently lowering his hands, 'is it you, the *amigo* of Señor Doc?'

Medway let the Mexican's hand actually touch his gun butt, then snapped two shots into his chest. Sanchez jerked backwards, writhing like a back-broken snake. He opened his mouth, trying to speak then jerked and was still. Without a glance at his victim, Medway rose and faded into the darkness.

Domingo was getting worried. He had heard nothing after those two pistols shots. After all, there was only one gringo.

Anxiously, he scanned the darkness, before suddenly expelling a huge sigh of relief as he saw a figure, wearing Cruzes' sombrero, walking towards him out of the shadows.

'You got him, then?' the young man demanded, as the figure halted an arm's length away.

Cruzes shook his head and said in Medway's voice, 'No, he got all three of us,' and the young man stared in disbelief as the hat was thrown back to reveal the features of the man they had been sent to kill. A grim little smile played around the Ranger's lips as he said, 'Those *hombres* got what they deserved, but it'd be best

46

if you just shuck that belt now.'

For a moment the youngster seemed to hesitate, then a slow answering smile spread across his features and he shrugged, before explaining, 'They were my *compañeros*. And for a man of honour . . . you see how it is, *señor*.' And as the last word left his lips, Domingo's hand blurred towards the pistol in his belt.

But he had barely begun to lift the weapon when Medway's bullet smashed into his chest, knocking him backwards and causing him to lose his grip on the Colt. Instantly, Medway was standing over him, poised for a second shot, but even as he watched, the boy's eyes glazed over and he slumped sideways.

Momentarily, Medway's face stiffened like granite, then he shrugged and reached down to touch the still face and close the staring eyes.

'Couldn't take no chances with a good man like you,' he explained gently, reaching down for the boy's six-gun. He made to toss it into the brush, then thought better of it and gave the weapon a quick examination.

'Not bad,' he muttered. 'I'm figgerin' I know another kid who'll die afore he'll run. Mebbe he can use this.' He sighed, adding, 'Though if'n he goes against Doc I'm probably just signing his death warrant.' He paused, looking over the equipment on the camp ground. His eye caught the shovel sticking out of Sanchez' untidy saddle pack and he grimaced.

'Them others'll do for buzzard bait but I'm sayin' the kid deserves a hole.' He scrubbed ruefully at his short hair, before adding, 'Even if I've got to dig it.'

CHAPTER SIX

Medway pulled gently on the reins and Cocoa came to a halt, dropping a tired head between her knees. The Ranger patted a dusty shoulder.

'Nearly there, ol' girl,' he offered, glancing ahead to where the lights of Paesar Querte battled against the dawn. Gently, he lifted the reins and Cocoa moved obediently forward. 'Hay and a stall for you,' he went on, 'and steak and a bed for me.' He grimaced, 'I sure hope them fellas stay lost.'

It had taken an hour of hard digging to inter the boy and Medway had been glad to saddle up and ride on. He'd left the main trail and followed a big circle through most of the night, finally arriving at his destination as the sun was rising.

Briefly, as he followed the sloping trail, he thought about his decision to leave the hacienda. On balance, he'd been right. It had been in character for the money-hungry desperado he was playing to make a play like that and Medina's ranch was just a mite too full of places which were ideal for pot shooting in the dark for comfort.

And if he'd stayed much longer, Medway knew he'd not have been able to stop himself shooting that greaser bastard Medina full of holes. To a Ranger, the job had to come first, so Lucy's killer would have to wait. But not for long, Medway acknowledged.

He found a small livery stable on the outskirts of town and with Cocoa groomed and chomping her slow way through a good feed of oats, Medway went in search of his own breakfast.

Next to the swinging doors of a big clapboard built saloon on the squalid main street, hung a sign reading GUDE EATS HEER, while, on the other side of the doorway a dapper little man in buckskins and moccasins was turning down a solitary oil-lamp.

Painfully aware of his depleted pockets, Medway said, 'What you chargin' for breakfast, *amigo*?'

'Give you a good big steak and fixin's for a dollar,' the little man answered, without looking round.

Medway grimaced. 'Ain't dealin' in shoe leather as well, are you?' he asked slyly.

Colour leapt up the little man's face and he glared at the Ranger before snapping, 'When I say a good steak,' he replied, 'I mean good!' Seeing the smile on his customer's face, he subsided, and extended a small, leathery hand. 'Name's Lucas Patton,' he offered, with a grin, 'but most folks call me Snuffy on account of I got kind of a short fuse.'

Medway shook the proffered hand and said gently, 'Bet I'd be kinda short if I had to eat my own cooking.'

This time the little man smiled and shook his head, 'You'd lose, *amigo*,' he stated emphatically, 'Mex or Yankee, my grub's good. Tell you what,' he went on, 'if'n it ain't the best steak you've eaten in a long while, I won't charge you nothing. How's that?'

'You got a bet,' Medway said wearily, following Patton inside.

'So?' Patton demanded, looking smugly at Medway's empty plate. His customer belched richly.

'You win,' Medway admitted sleepily, proffering a dollar from his dwindling supply. 'Now all I need is a clean bed and after that, mebbe a little game to pass the time.'

Patton's face lost its grin.

'I wouldn't have took you for a card sh— gambler,' he amended quickly.

Medway shrugged. 'I cut loose from my ol' place after the fall round-up,' he began smoothly. 'Had three months' pay in my jeans, figgered to see some country. I like to play poker and you wouldn't believe the number o' fellas between here and the Canadian line who think they can play stud hoss and can't.'

Medway's smile was frank but the little saloon keeper said grimly, 'I'd advise you against playing cards in this town.' Medway raised an eyebrow, and the other continued, 'Strangers allus lose . . . one way or another.'

Looking over the customers in Patton's saloon that night, Medway wondered if the little man had been joking. There was no sign of anything or anyone out of the ordinary as Medway advanced to the bar and raised his hand in the age-old gesture.

'Go easy on that stuff,' Patton warned, as Medway

sipped and nodded appreciatively.

Looking up at the little man from under his hat brim, Medway said gently, 'She seems plumb peaceful to me, old-timer. Sure you ain't trying throw a scare into a poor li'l pilgrim?'

Patton looked him over in disgust. 'You'll learn,' he said shortly.

The lesson began some little time later. Medway had eased himself into a quiet game and had been winning steadily, if unspectacularly, when the evening's peace was shattered by a young man lurching violently through the swing doors and smashing into the bar, to be almost instantly followed by four others of about the same age.

Reaching out a meaty hand, the largest of the group was about to grasp the youngster's shirt front, when a sharp double click from behind the bar drew his attention. He looked up into a pair of icy-grey eyes above the twin tubes of a sawn-off shotgun and Lucas Patton's voice was saying crisply, 'Not in my place. You want to drink or play, sit down. But nothin' else. Nothin'. You understand me, Bucky?'

For a moment, it looked like trouble, then the big youngster grinned and said, 'Sure, Snuffy, we don't want no trouble. Just teachin' Brad here some manners.' To the young man on the floor, he said, 'I'll be callin' on your sister tomorrow. Better make sure she's feelin' sociable.'

'She'd sooner associate with a skunk,' the other snapped, flinching as his tormentor raised a hand.

'I don't tell no one twice,' Patton stated softly, but

his voice cut like a file as he continued, 'Likewise, it's "Mr Patton" to you, Bucky, and if'n you don't think I mean what I say, you little bastard, touch that boy agin.' The twin barrels lifted slightly and Patton added, 'Try, if you think you're good enough, Thad.'

The man behind the one called Bucky jerked his hand away from his Colt as though it had suddenly become red hot and Patton grinned mirthlessly. Another jerk of his weapon sent the group around the bar away from the injured boy, who dragged himself to his feet and staggered into the night while Medway slipped his left-hand Colt back into his lap. Obviously, Snuffy Patton and trouble were old acquaintances.

'You pay for any drinks now,' Patton stated to the fuming Bucky. 'No credit and you leave your guns here,' he finished pointing to the bar top.

'What the . . .' Bucky began but the twin barrels lifted again and he subsided grumbling as he stripped his twin-holstered belt, while ordering his companions to do the same.

The room seemed to breathe a collective sigh of relief as the group moved away from the bar and headed towards an empty table. All except Bucky, that is, who, whiskey bottle and glass in hand, lurched to a stop in front of the table where Medway had just begun to deal and demanded, 'Wha' you playing?'

'Stud,' one of the others offered nervously.

Bucky placed a hand on the shoulder of nearest man and said, 'I'll sit in. Ol' Frank here ought to be gettin' home anyways.' The man addressed looked up and scowled before nodding tightly. 'Guess I'm a little tired at that,' he said weakly, and rose to go, making as if to scoop up his winnings, only to stop as the bully said, 'Don' worry, Frank. I'll take care o' your chips.' For a moment, the other looked like he might object, then he flushed and turned away angrily.

Bucky slid into the vacant seat, glaring pointedly at Medway before saying arrogantly, 'I'm Buck De Grace and my pa owns this flea-bitten town and everything in it. And everyone. Deal me some cards.'

Medway dealt himself a second card face up, looked up and said softly, 'King bets. You're in next round, kid, an' don't make me explain why.'

Play around the table now became sporadic and it soon became plain to Medway that what De Grace knew about stud poker would have gone on the back of a postage stamp. A very small postage stamp.

He stayed in for almost every hand, seemed to have unlimited faith in his ability to fill any straight or flush, no matter where the cards lay or what had gone before. Medway, for whom poker amounted to something like an exact science, found his frustration growing, and when, for what seemed like the thousandth time, De Grace flung down his cards and cursed his luck, Medway said shortly, 'It ain't bad luck, it's bad play.'

De Grace looked up from the glass he had just filled with whiskey. 'Wha' did you say, you goddamn saddle bum?' he slurred.

'I said, you play poker like a cow and if'n you wasn't livin' on your daddy's muscle, no one'd let you near a table,' the Ranger stated flatly.

Slipping away his nearside Colt, Medway rose and scooped his winnings into his hat.

De Grace watched him for a moment, then snapped in drunken irritation, 'Hold it, mister. You ain't leaving this table till I've had a chance to get my money back.'

Medway transferred the coin-laden hat to his head dexterously then sighed and said. 'I'd have to sit here about twenty years afore you learned enough poker to get a cent o' this coin back. And I ain't got that long.' Across the bar-room, Medway saw the hand of the one Patton had called Thad stealing towards the open flap of his coat.

Before anyone could move, De Grace grabbed the edge of the table and threw it aside. As the table flew past him, Medway stepped gracefully around it and before the big man could prevent it, Medway's fist shot past his guard and smashed into his nose. De Grace's hands flew to his injured face and Medway hammered a swift punch into the man's stomach, following up with a massive uppercut that slammed in to De Grace's chin and deposited him, stunned and bleeding, on the sawdust-covered floor.

Even before his victim hit the grimy boards, Medway's hand dipped and there was a Colt roaring in his fist. His first shot caught Thad high in the chest, knocking him sideways and causing him to drop his weapon. Cautiously, Medway moved forward kicking the pistol away before bending to examine his second victim, ready for another shot.

It wasn't needed and Medway had just decided that his victim might even live when a flat, even voice said boredly, 'Unless you want a hole where nature never intended you to have a hole, cowboy, put both them pistols on the floor and stand up slow with your hands on your hat.' Medway knew that tone of voice, so he complied very carefully, finally straightening up to obey the last order.

Roughly, a calloused hand thoroughly searched his clothing, then a new voice said diffidently, 'He's clean Jake . . . I-I mean Marshal.'

'Turn around,' said the first voice, adding not unkindly, 'Then you can put your hands down and tell me your side of it.'

Medway found himself facing a pair of peace offi-cers almost unique in his experience. One was short and slim, dressed in a plain, neat broadcloth suit on which was pinned the star of a town marshal and he was carrying a battered ten gauge which he handled with the accomplished air of an expert. By contrast, his companion, was old, thin as a picket rail and his face wore a look of bemused anxiety. Medway, however, wasn't fooled. His twin belts hung just right and the smooth-butted Colts in their worn, tied-down holsters had seen a lot of use.

'So what happened here, stranger?' the marshal asked reasonably. 'And,' he interrupted as one of De Grace's remaining companions began to protest, 'I'll listen to you in a minute.'

Briefly, Medway explained what had happened and when he had finished, his questioner cocked an eye at Patton.

'Just like he said,' the saloon-keeper agreed, nodding towards a glowering and fully conscious De Grace. 'Bucky pushed his luck too far once too often. He's bin' askin' fer it long enough, Jake, I don't need to tell you and Yancy that,' he finished, grinning at the deputy who was staring bemusedly into the bottom of a half-empty whiskey glass. The older man shrugged.

'Looks like a clear case o' self-defence to me, Jake ' he offered nervously. The other nodded, reaching down for Medway's Colts.

'Sounds like you're in the clear, stranger,' he began easily, proffering the weapons, with his back to De Grace's companions. 'I'm Brady, Town Marshal, as you've probably guessed.' He grinned, tapping the badge with the muzzles of the ten gauge, still clutched in a slim hand. 'And the old fossil is my deppity.'

Without taking his eyes from De Grace's companions, the old man raised his glass and said, 'Sumers, Yance Sumers.' For a split second, the deputy's searching gaze swept across Medway and his equipment, then he said diffidently, 'Pleased to know you, son.'

'Likewise,' Medway answered gently.

Without warning, Buck De Grace surged to his feet and stormed across the room to stand almost nose to nose with the marshal.

'Ain't you gonna do nothin'?' he snapped. 'When one o' this fleabag town's best customers gets stomped by a nobody, you figger to jest let him get away with it? Goddamit, you better arrest him, Brady!'

CHAPTER SEVEN

Jake Brady's answer was simple.

The butt of the ten gauge smashed down on De Grace's toe and, as the bully leant forward, howling with pain, Brady slapped the breech of the weapon into his already discoloured and swollen nose. Bucky subsided, screaming and any attempt at interference by his companions came to an abrupt end when they found themselves looking into the muzzles of Yance Sumers's twin Colts.

'You ain't anywhere close to bein' a respected member o' this community,' Brady said softly. 'You're a worthless piece o' trash no decent man'd wipe his boots on. Get him outa here.'

'I ain't forgettin' this, Brady,' De Grace screamed past the blood that dribbled into his mouth. He spat a spray of crimson. 'And I ain't fergettin' you either, saddle bum,' he snapped as his companions half led, half carried him through the swing doors in the direction of the doctor's office.

Softly, Sumers sidled up to the opening, briefly examined the night-time street and only then did he slide his Colts away. Turning to Medway, he offered gently, 'I'd say that rattler don't like you.'

'I'm sure losin' sleep over it,' came the terse reply.

Losing sleep or not, Buck De Grace wasn't one to leave a debt unpaid, unless, of course, it involved him spending money. Or rather his Daddy's money.

So it was, that, three days later, he and his three companions were huddled over warm glasses of beer, all they could afford after their spree had run its course, cursing the world in general and a certain cowboy called Medway in particular. None of them noticed the slim, black-dressed young man with the babyish face who sat at an adjacent table.

Doc's ears perked up as De Grace said, 'I ain't leavin' till I'm square with that bastard Medway.'

'I'm agreein' with them general sentiments,' Thad offered, 'But how we gonna do it? Brady's took our guns an', anyhow, I ain't in the mood to stack up against that coyote unless we got some sort of an edge. He's too handy.'

Above the murmur of grudging acquiescence, Bucky snapped, 'Don't worry. I got a plan. We'll borrow some guns then . . .'

Doc grinned as Bucky laid out his plan. He'd need another to help him, certainly, someone trustworthy. Then his smile broadened. Of course, he would be the very man.

Later that evening, as he strolled through the sprawling Mexican quarter of the little border town, Medway heard a woman scream. Of course, he should have known better and, as he slipped a Colt from its holster and sprinted around a nearby corner, intent on locating the author of the noise, he met a pistol barrel coming the other way. He slumped, barely conscious, hardly feeling it as his jacket was jerked off and his hands and feet tied quickly and efficiently. Through the mud that seemed to be clogging his brain, he heard a familiar voice say, 'Leave him, he ain't goin' nowhere.'

'Quite,' snapped another. 'But don't waste any time doing your part!'

There was a pause and the first voice said, 'Yeah, but I'm figgering on a little insurance.'

There was a swift scuffle then the second voice said breathlessly, 'Give me back that gun, Drago, you son of a bitch!'

'Sure,' the outlaw said coolly, 'when I've . . .' But the blackness beckoned and Medway slipped away into unconsciousness and knew no more.

Not, that is, until he awoke to the familiar pounding in his skull and the feeling that, this time, he'd maybe made a bad mistake in underestimating the opposition.

Carefully, he opened one eye and examined his surroundings. He was lying in an alley, between two adobe buildings. His hands and feet were free and he still had his guns, while his battered denim jacket lay nearby. Dragging on his hat, he managed to stand at the third attempt and headed towards the nearby saloon. It was a puzzle, because Medway had expected to wake up dead and he couldn't figure out why he hadn't.

Patton's saloon was open, as usual, and Medway staggered through the doors and fetched up against the bar. Patton came forward himself to serve the Ranger, only to recoil as he caught a whiff of Medway's clothes.

'You must have surely tied one on last night, boy,' Patton stated, as he poured liquor into a glass and handed it across the bar, 'and I'm sure admittin' you got some nerve comin' back here.'

'How's that,' Medway asked weakly, pushing aside the drink and holding his aching temples. 'I—'

'Shot my pard Bucky in the back, you sonovabitch,' came Thad's caustic interruption. 'But now you're gonna get yours!'

If the killer had fired without speaking, he would probably have lived. As it was, he was barely halfway through his diatribe before Medway had twisted, dropped to the sawdust strewn floor and palmed a Colt. Thad's first shot chopped through the timber of the bar inches above Medway's head as the Ranger's hand blurred over the hammer, emptying the Colt into his opponent's body.

Caught in the hail of .44 slugs, Thad was thrown backwards, knocking aside a table and landing on the floor where his body thrashed out its last few seconds of life. From the floor, Medway could see none of this and his second pistol was in his hand before he demanded, 'He cashed?'

Patton moved carefully around the table and lifted the body with a boot toe.

'Well,' the saloon-keeper said callously, 'if'n he ain't a corpse, I ain't never seen one.'

He looked up, then froze as a mild voice behind Medway said, 'In any other town you'd get a vote of thanks for killin' vermin like that. Best you get rid o' them guns, boy.'

Carefully, Medway complied, before demanding, as Yance Sumers booted the weapons aside and motioned to him to rise, 'What in hell is this? Why'd that fool try to kill me?'

Sumers shrugged. 'I ain't right sure,' he offered diffidently, 'but it might have something to do with you blowin' the back o' Bucky's head off last night.' He motioned negligently with a Colt-filled hand towards a table against the back wall, 'Ol' Lucas ain't even cleaned the blood up good yet.'

'Fer Chris'sake,' Medway began, for what seemed like the millionth time, 'I already told you. I got jumped; they tied me up. I come to this mornin' with a head ache and went lookin' for somethin' to fix it. That's all.' Jake Brady whistled sceptically and fingered the badge pinned to his shirt.

'Hard to believe,' he began. 'I ain't never heard of anybody being jumped just fer the exercise. You sure there's nothin' missin'?'

Medway nodded, but before he could open his mouth, Yance Sumers hissed from the front window, 'Jake! It's 'Lonzo De Grace, with his outfit and they don't look like they come for a church social!'

Instantly, Brady was at the window and his hard gaze took in the scene. Alonzo De Grace was riding his favourite piebald down the middle of the moonlit main street as though he owned it, followed by a bunch of his toughest men. Opposite Lucas Patton's Painted Lady saloon, he dismounted and stamped up the entrance steps, followed by his men.

'I don't figger he'll start nothin' hisself,' Sumers offered shrewdly. 'He'll likely try and get some o' the town yellin' rope first, and leave hisself a free hand to take it from there.' Seeing his young boss's lips tighten as he looked towards the rear door, Sumers forestalled him.

'He's bound to be watching both trails outa town, son,' the old man offered gently.

Brady sighed and nodded. 'Figgered that my own self, Yance,' he admitted, glancing across at Medway, who seemed wholly concerned with the construction of a cigarette. Inconsequentially, the younger man demanded, 'He strike you as the sort to be a back-shooter?'

'Wondered how long it'd take ye,' the old man admitted. 'No, and it don't make sense, 'cause I figger that boy coulda give Bucky and his *amigos* about two weeks' start and still killed all of 'em before any of 'em had cleared leather.'

In the saloon, Doc felt the whiskey-fuelled belligerence of the crowd growing. Turning to the filthy white man at his side, he ordered, 'Get out and make sure everything's ready. And Murdoch,' he finished, as the man rose to go, 'no mistakes. Understand?'

Nervously the man nodded and left by the rear door. Doc gave him a full minute before rising himself and exiting via the batwings. Pausing on the front step, he lit an expensive cheroot and sauntered towards the jail, angling across the street to pass behind the building.

Yance slapped the red two down on the black three and leaned back with a self-satisfied smirk.

'First one I've got out in a year,' he crowed, as Brady leaned over his shoulder, studying the spread of cards.

The younger man grinned and said, 'You've done it agin, you ol' fossil. You know you can't put a black queen on—' Whatever Brady was about to say was lost in the thunderous banging on the massive front door of the jailhouse.

Sumers reached down and turned down the lamp he had hidden behind the desk, while Brady slipped along the wall and peered through the lower pane of the nearest window. His finger moved rapidly, signalling one man on the porch, while others were visible in the street. His next finger twitch sent Sumers to the rifle rack then gliding out the rear exit. Having allowed his deputy some minutes to reach the prearranged position, Brady interrupted Alonzo De Grace's stentorian bellow by the simple expedient of opening the visitors' flap in the door and shoving a piece of ordnance, familiarly known as a sawn-off shotgun, almost up that worthy's nose.

'What d'you want?' Brady snapped, as the disconcerted De Grace stepped back. 'And whatever it is,' the young man added, 'keep your cotton-pickin' hands still!'

De Grace, who had been fumbling for a handkerchief immediately jerked his hands shoulder high and thundered, 'Goddammit, Brady, you know what we

want! I come for that sonovabitch who killed my B—'
But the rest of the cattleman's words were lost in the
blast of a tremendous explosion, which tore the back
off of the De Grace Emporium and General Store.

For a moment there was stunned silence, then De
Grace was bellowing incomprehensibly and leaping
into the street. He tore the reins loose and was about
to shove a leg into the stirrup when there was the
crack of a shot. De Grace slumped forward against his
saddle and a voice from the darkness screamed, 'Don'
shoot, deppity, you've hit the boss!'

For an instant, there was silence. Then big Rance
Crowther, foreman of De Grace's enormous D bar G
spread bellowed, 'Git 'em, boys!' and dropped one
enormous hand to his holstered pistol. He never
pulled because, ahead of all of them, Yance Sumers's
Colt leapt into view and his first shot tore a foot-long
furrow in the flank of Crowther's pony.

Maddened beyond all control, the savage little beast
sprang sideways, unseating his rider and causing chaos
amongst the remaining D bar G riders, their confu-
sion added to by a shotgun blast that tore the air to
pieces above their heads.

Into this bedlam of men and animals strode old
Yance Sumers and hands that had been straying to
pistol butts were stilled because this agate-eyed demon
bore no resemblance to the mild deputy the D bar G
boys treated to drinks every pay day. The old man
halted beside Crowther and the big man, no coward
himself, swallowed hard and fervently wished himself
somewhere else. He'd been in town that day when this
old six-gun wizard had taken on the four Hardin boys

and killed all of them without receiving a shot in return. So he lay very still as Sumers snapped, 'Get up and see to your hoss and your boss, whichever way round you like. Where's Jake? And in case any o' you yahoos ain't clear about it, I'll kill the first man who touches a gun.'

The D bar G crew instantly forgot, to a man, that they were carrying weapons.

To his boss, the old man said, 'Marshal, you better check the prisoner.'

From the door of the jail there came a disgusted grunt.

What prisoner?'

Sumers sighed and the diffident old man was back.

'Guess I shoulda figgered,' he offered to no one in particular.

CHAPTER EIGHT

It had been done mighty slickly, even Medway was forced to admit that as he signalled Cocoa to a halt on the Mexican bank of the Rio Grande.

He'd heard the dull crump of the explosion and even before his ears had stopped ringing, Drago and another man had appeared through the rear door. Without ;a sound or wasted motion, they had opened the cell door and thrust Medway's weapon belt into his hands.

Still in silence, and ignoring the uproar and shooting on Main Street, the three men had slipped out of the jail and come, by a series of winding alleyways, to a small corral where Cocoa and several other horses waited.

Cocoa nickered her welcome before viciously snapping at the man holding her bridle. He released her with a yelp and she trotted forward contentedly nuzzling for sugar at Medway's pocket.

'Glad you're here to look after that li'l goat,' Drago laughed with uncharacteristic good humour. 'She near chewed Diego's arm off when he tried to saddle her,' he finished, nodding at the disgruntled Mexican.

Medway nodded in turn. 'Just so's it is clear, *amigos*,'

he said, in his fluid border Spanish, 'if *la señora* don't kill the next one who touches her . . . I will.'

It had been a neat touch of ingratitude, wholly in character for a vicious gringo, Medway thought as he watched the bunch of scowling greasers file past him. Doc had joined them as the sun moved into the afternoon. He was surprisingly cheerful, considering the news he brought.

'Posse following,' he began brightly.

'Goddammit,' Drago flared, then immediately calmed. 'Hell, it won't matter. They got no jurisdiction in Mexico,' he finished uncertainly.

Medway gave a crow of laughter. 'If you think that,' he snapped, 'you don't know Texas lawmen.'

'Some of us mebbe don't savvy lawdogs the way you do,' Drago spat waspishly, but before Medway could develop the argument, Doc interrupted.

'This isn't helping,' he snapped priggishly. 'Gonzalez says they're only a couple of hours behind us.'

Drago spat viciously. 'Hell, it's pretty simple,' he said, 'we either got to lose them or kill 'em. No other way.' He thought for a moment, then swung the big bay up the trail. 'I know just the place,' he stated, as the others moved alongside him. 'Coupla hours from here, there's a little box canyon. Looks OK at the start, but she gets real narrow, real quick. And,' he finished significantly, 'you can't see it's blind till you're right inside.'

'I like it,' Doc sniggered. 'We'll lay a false trail, then when those fools follow it in, we can finish them, like rats in a trap. What d'you think, Medway?' he snapped suddenly.

Caught unawares Medway managed a tight smile before saying, 'Sounds good to me.'

Doc nodded, as though satisfied and the Ranger let the two men move ahead as his mind raced, desperate to form a plan that would prevent the massacre.

Medway still hadn't come up with anything by the time they reached the canyon, only to find that, if anything, Drago had underestimated its potential as an ambush site.

Rock walls rose sheer from their base, lining the narrow trail, until, after about a hundred feet, they angled back and became littered with scree and larger boulders, providing plenty of cover for the attackers, while leaving anyone in the narrow ravine a sitting target, with no effective shelter for several hundred yards.

The only chance Medway could see was sunset, which a glance at the sky told him was barely an hour away. As if in echo to his thought, Drago said, as he swung out of the saddle, 'They ain't gonna come tonight, but just in case,' he went on, indicating both slopes in turn, 'Doc, take some boys up there. Me an' Medway'll camp on the other side. Remember, don't let none of the bastards escape.'

As Drago made to turn away, Doc snapped, 'It's a good plan except for one thing: Medway comes with me.' The black-dressed killer's hand hung ready over the butt of his fancy Colt and Drago raised an eyebrow in response.

'Trustin' li'l fella, ain't you?' he said quizzically.

'It comes from having too many dealings with scum,' came the acid reply.

'You, Medway,' Doc went on, ignoring the smouldering Drago, 'Get your gear. We're camping out up there and you better stay where I can see you!'

It wasn't until later that night when the ambushers were comfortably settled in their blankets that the idea popped fully formed into Medway's brain. It was a long shot but it looked like that or nothing. His other problem lay in getting out of camp without arousing suspicion. Then he smiled. There was, of course, always the age-old problem Mexico kept in store for travellers.

Slowly, Medway began to wriggle and squirm in his blankets, periodically letting out a low moan. Suddenly, he jerked back the covers and sat up only to find himself looking down the muzzle of a .38.

'Where are you going?' Doc snapped peevishly.

Medway set his face into a mask of agony. 'Them beans . . . I-I . . . they ain't settin' right. I got to go. . . .' But the last was flung over his shoulder as he vanished into the darkness.

In five minutes, he was back. And ten minutes after that, the blankets were flung off and Medway disappeared again into the darkness. Doc barely stirred and, on his return, Medway slipped down into his quilts and set himself to wait until the black-dressed killer was firmly asleep. This time, he rose silently, and leaving his hat on the saddle and a fold of blanket to simulate his body, he slipped down towards the trail, carefully collecting a handful of sun-dried sticks as he went.

'I don't like it,' Yance Sumers stated categorically. 'I

know the country they're headin' for and I'm tellin' you, Jake, if'n there's a better place for ambushes on God's earth I never heerd tell of it!'

Sumers and Brady, along with a motley collection of townsmen, had been following the bandidos' trail since sun-up. It was plain enough for even Brady to read, but something had been nagging at the old deputy for a while now. Something about those pony tracks . . .

Suddenly, Sumers jerked his pony to a halt. In the centre of the trail, someone had constructed a circle of sticks and in the centre had been placed a large rock.

Hand caressing the stock of his Winchester, the old man stared down at the message of the sticks. Brady jerked him out of his reverie.

'What we waitin' on, Yance?' the younger man demanded impatiently, as he pulled up at his deputy's side.

'Don't make it obvious,' Sumers ordered, matter-of-factly. 'Just look down.' Leaning back, the old man unhooked his canteen and took a small drink that he didn't really want.

'That circle of sticks with the rock in the middle is Indian sign,' Sumers went on, as he made a show of recorking the canteen and gathering the reins. 'It means go back to camp and now I think about it, some o' them ponies we been following ain't carrying weight.' Bleakly, he examined the walls of the canyon ahead, and gave a grunt of satisfaction as he saw them begin to rise sheer a bare hundred yards ahead.

'They nearly caught us, Jake boy,' Sumers began, continuing before the bemused young man could interrupt, 'When I yell, you turn your pony and high-tail it back the way we come.'

Sunlight glinted high on the canyon wall ahead, and Sumers bellowed, 'Now'd be a real good time.' Dragging his pony around, he dug spurs into the startled little beast.

The rest of the posse needed no second urging, because even as Sumers spurred his mount to a dead run, there was a fusillade of shots and Brady's pony gave a grunt and slewed sideways at full gallop, throwing the young marshal headlong.

His companions thundered on unhit, all that is except Yance Sumers, who dragged his pony around in a wide circle and headed back for the stunned Brady.

Up on the rim rock, Doc drew a careful bead, then snapped his rifle up, because suddenly, Yance Sumers's mustang appeared to have no rider. Medway, positioned slightly further forward, grinned as he watched the old man, hanging from the horn of his saddle Comanche-style, jerk a stunned Brady across the pommel and swing back again for the safety of the rocks which the rest of his party had already reached, the game little mustang stretching out to full gallop despite his double burden and the hail of bullets which accompanied him.

'Goddamn that old bastard!' Doc snarled, carelessly throwing down the rifle he'd been using. Mentally, Medway raised an eyebrow. In a land where a man depended upon his weapons being ready for instant use, only a fool treated them in such an offhand manner. That might be just another little thing in the good guy's favour.

'How in hell did he know we were waiting?' Doc's voice dropped ominously as he glared in Medway's direction. Knowing the black-dressed killer's twisted hatred for him, Medway shifted and dropped his hand casually beltwards. Salvation, however, came to the Ranger from an unexpected quarter.

'It was the ponies mebbe, *señor*,' began a quavering voice. Instantly Doc snapped round, pistol menacing the speaker.

'What d'you mean, you fat slug?' he roared.

'M-m-mebbe so he spot some of the ponies, they no got riders?' The terrified bandido managed a shrug. 'He was lookin' at the groun' when they run for it, *señor.*'

For a moment, the Mexican's life certainly hung in the balance then the insane rage left Doc's eyes and he lifted the pistol. A moment later, the weapon was holstered and Doc was bellowing, 'Saddle up. We're getting out of here.'

'Ain't no need to bother about them guys,' Drago sneered, in answer to Doc's question as the two groups swung on to the trail together.

'They're short a horse,' he went on, 'and we sure musta nicked a couple of 'em. Naw,' he finished, 'they'll scuttle out of these hills with their tails between their legs.' Medway nodded in agreement, but knowing something of the calibre of men like Brady and his elderly deputy, he was certain they wouldn't let the business rest there.

Medway shifted uneasily in the saddle as he watched night begin to fall on the trail ahead. He nudged the elbow of the man riding next to him and Drago turned his head lazily at Medway's prodding.

'We gonna camp tonight?' Medway demanded peevishly. Drago's teeth showed white against his night tinted face.

'Sure,' he answered, 'nice li'l town just up ahead. Good grub, clean beds, all a man wants. Nice clean gals too, if you want that.'

Half an hour later, Drago was proved right as Medway found himself riding through the gold of a Mexican dusk into a tiny adobe-built village.

People were going about their evening business with a casual placidity and, as Drago pulled up at the hitch rail of the tiny *cantina*, Medway took a swift glance around.

Down the street, two women were carrying home their tools and a basket of corn, their gleanings from the swiftly ripening fields, while behind them, another woman was turning a big, raw-boned mule into a sun-bleached adobe corral.

'Gonna see after my pony,' Medway flung over his shoulder, as he eased Cocoa down the street.

Sitting in the *cantina* that night, nursing one careful drink, Medway had a lot to think about. He'd circled the town, on the pretence of looking for a stable, and was confident he'd covered most of the place.

'So why in hell didn't I see one grown man anywhere?' he asked himself quizzically.

CHAPTER NINE

The journey back to the Medina hacienda didn't take long and it was late afternoon when Medway found himself once again sitting across the desk from the wheelchair-bound Wilson. The Easterner began without preamble.

'Glad to see you back, Mr Medway. I take it that my original offer is now acceptable and we won't hear any more about fifty dollars a day. I think you might be grateful to get out of that flea bag of a town alive,' Wilson finished venomously.

'Pickin's in somethin' this big sure sounds good to me,' Medway said sheepishly, breathing an inaudible sigh of relief that his cover was still intact. Clearly, Drago was saving him for something else.

'All right then,' Wilson went on smoothly. 'The plan is this: our revolutionary army will sweep through the southern parts of the United States, killing and burning, while a team of picked men, which will include you and your *friend* – the word drew a sneer to Wilson's razor-thin lips – 'follow behind and bust all the banks, stores, saloons, anywhere with money, bonds, deeds, things like that. Your ill-gotten gains will be brought here and we'll split the money, half to my Mexican backers and the other half between ourselves. How's it sound?'

Medway resisted his overwhelming desire to say, 'Madness', and answered instead, 'There's a lot of gold in them south-western banks all right, but it won't come to much if we're splitting with a coupla hundred greaser soldiers!'

Wilson shook his head. 'That isn't your worry. I'm calculatin' we stand to make about a hundred to two hundred thousand a piece, while the greasers get their country back. Well?'

'Sounds good,' Medway admitted, while wondering just how long a bunch of Mexican dreamers were liable to hold on to Texas land.

'But what about the deeds and bonds and such?'

'Again ... not your concern!' was the snapped reply. 'Are you in or not?'

'Oh, in, for sure,' Medway answered quickly. 'I sure like a game where a fella's got a choice,' he finished diffidently.

It was growing dark and Jose Negas was finishing up the last of his interminable chores, when a hand clamped over his mouth from behind and he was half dragged, half carried around a convenient corner. His attacker shoved him gently against the wall, keeping the hand in place before saying in Jim Medway's Texas drawl, 'Ssh, It's me. You remember? From the wagons?' A vigorous nod was his answer and he continued. 'I got somethin' you might find useful but I need some information.' There was another nod and Medway eased his hand away from the boy's mouth. He fumbled at his waist and then pushed the holstered Colt he had taken from the other boy into Negas's eager hands.

Barely able to contain his joy, Negas still had sense enough to make no noise as Medway went on, 'Tell me how you first came here.'

For a moment the boy's face twisted, then he said, 'The man in black, he came to my village with men with guns. They herded us, my father and brothers and me, drove us like cattle to a place in the mountains. There is a gold mine, *señor*, that is where they make us work.'

Medway nodded grimly at finding his suspicions confirmed.

'I need to know where these people are keeping your friends,' the Ranger said gently, 'and the other people from your village.'

Negas shrugged in the darkness. 'I cannot tell you, *señor*,' he admitted. 'The wagons that leave from here, they are always covered until we get to the camp.'

Medway thought a moment then asked, 'How long to get there?'

'A day and part of the night.' Negas shrugged. 'There is no food and water until we reach the camp. Everyone is verra thirsty.'

'Tell me about the camp,' Medway demanded thoughtfully. 'I mebbe know a coupla fellas who are just right for a job like this.'

In a pair of long and largely misspent lives, Slim and

76

Shorty had had more than their fair share of uninvited night-time visitors, usually large, vicious individuals intent on blowing or cutting large holes in one or both of them.

So when a board creaked tn the ramshackle veranda that ran across the front of their borrowed dwelling, Slim simply flicked open one eye, saw a tall shadow that was his partner moving to crouch behind the door, and felt for his pistol.

Wide awake now, eyes drawn to slits, Slim turned luxuriously, contriving to silently move his gun from under the frowzy pillow he was using to his blanket.

Silently, the door swung open and Slim waited for a sight of their visitor. But none appeared and Slim lay immobile, eyes straining through the darkness. Suddenly, there was a whisper of sound, a creaking sigh from the floor nearby and Slim relaxed. Gradually, a rounded shadow crept over the edge of the bed turning slowly into the hatless silhouette of a man.

Before the other could move, Slim's Colt was boring into his chest and the little man was hissing cheerfully, '*Saludos, amigo.* Now you set right still and nobody's gonna get hurt. Especially you,' Slim added meaningfully.

'He ain't got no friends,' came Shorty's voice from the half-open doorway. 'Strike a light, Slim,' the tall one went on, 'so's we kin see what we catched.'

'Don't you go strikin' no goddamn matches with me around,' their visitor snapped, in a voice both men knew well.

'Jim! Well, I'll be damned. What you sneakin' in

here fer?' Shorty demanded.

' 'Cause he wants to advertise that he knows us, you goddamn long streak o' stupidity,' Slim snapped, quicker on the uptake than his friend. Peering through the darkness, he demanded, 'What's up?'

'Plenty,' came the peevish reply. 'So listen close 'cause I ain't got time to say this twice.'

'So what d'you think,' Medway demanded, when his explanations were all finished.

'Shouldn't be hard,' Slim said judiciously. 'Kid said they was using a mesa top to pen these greasers?' he asked, and sensing rather than seeing Medway's confirmation, went on, 'Can't be that many big enough and with reliable water within a day's ride. We'll find it easy.'

'How you figger to get out without someone spottin' you?' Medway asked.

Shorty chuckled in the darkness. 'That's easy. We'll leave our ponies in the corral and just liberate us a couple from Medina's herd. People allus see what they expect to see,' he explained. ' 'Cause our mounts are here, why, so are we. Why you so interested in these greasers, anyhow, Jim?'

'I'm recruitin',' came the flat answer.

There followed a tense couple of days for Jim Medway. Wilson had let slip that he expected the nucleus of his rebel army very soon and if Slim and Shorty couldn't find the peon camp, his plans would have to change radically.

So it was with a sinking heart that the Ranger heard

the yell that followed a racing rider into the main square of the hacienda.

'The Mexicans! Tortuga's coming!'

So it proved.

Heading the cavalcade of riders was a tall, scar-faced Mexican, dressed in the height of *caballero* fashion and riding a magnificent palomino stallion. Behind him, on a sorrel nearly as good, paced a giant, heavily muscled Negro, hatless and apparently without any weapon except a long bladed machete in a sheath covered with Chiricahua beadwork. Behind this ornamental pair rode a collection of ragged, mostly barefoot Mexicans. Many of them were weaponless apart from the occasional rusting pistol or rifle.

Medway was about to follow the motley collection down the street, when a hated voice said, 'How you like our leetle army, Señor Safe Cracker?'

Medway shrugged, strangling down the blind hatred that threatened to engulf him and said casually, 'Least none of 'em look yeller, Medina.'

There was a sharp intake of breath as Medway went on, 'Who's the jay bird with the fancy yeller pony?'

For a moment, it seemed as if the hacienda owner would refuse to answer but finally he snapped, 'His name is Tortuga, Orsino Tortuga and you better stay away from that horse. He thinks more of it than his *madre*! On second thoughts, gringo, don't stay away! Fool wi't him all you wan',' Medina finished viciously as he turned on his heel and stalked away. Medway glanced after the fuming Mexican but, for once, his thoughts did not run on the five or six excessively painful ways he had thought up for killing Georges Medina.

'Mebbe somebody oughta play a little game with those fellas,' he mused, 'just to kinda keep 'em interested.'

'Yeah, we know ol' Orsino,' Shorty admitted, 'but he don' like us.'

The oldsters had just returned and the three men were occupying a dark table in the back of the deserted *cantina*.

'I bet you lose sleep over that,' Medway offered waspishly, but Slim shook his head.

'Nary a wink,' he said, 'but how come you know him, Jim?'

'Saw him ride in this morning,' the Ranger replied. 'But what about this camp? D'you manage to find it?'

'Sure, just like the kid said, high on a mesa, good water, guards, the whole thing. Only . . .' Slim paused and his partner continued.

'Sure funny about them guards.' Medway looked his question and Shorty went on thoughtfully. 'They wasn't your usual Americano *pistoleros*. They was more like soldiers, cavalry men. Had cavalry holsters and guns, too.'

Medway shrugged. 'Plenty of ex-army men workin' below the line,' he said.

Shorty looked carefully around the crowded *cantina* before dropping his voice and saying, 'Sure, but those are all ex-army. We checked their mounts. Cavalry brands every one and not vented.'

Medway whistled. 'Deserters?' he suggested.

Shorty shrugged vaguely and Slim said, 'Nope. Too much discipline, and if the fella they was all takin' orders from ain't a thirty-year top soldier, I ain't never seen one! And there's somethin else,' Slim went on. 'We found the mine and in a li'l cave tucked out the way, somebody got the biggest stash o' guns I ever seen. Including,' he went on, as Medway's eyes widened, 'three o' the latest model Gatling guns! Now you tell me,' the tall one continued, 'what in hell use is a gun you gotta wagon mount to a horse Injun?'

For some moments. Medway thought quickly, while Slim and Shorty scanned the gathering crowd.

'We oughta get out of here,' Slim began. 'If Drago or one o' them others sees us . . .'

'OK,' Medway began quickly, gathering up the scattered cards and pretending to deal a hand. 'I can't figger where the Gatlings come in all this but I sure as hell can guess who them rifles are for. This is what we do. Vittorio and his boys are due in tomorrow, sometime before sundown. Wilson's anxious, now everything's in place, to get movin', I'll bet, so he'll let the Indians and the greasers know what his plan is sometime day after tomorrow so's he can get them on their way, with yours truly and the others following along behind. That means,' the Ranger went on, 'he'll want them guns here by tomorrow night. I'll arrange a li'l diversion to keep 'em back for a day or two and you two can get out to the mine and put a crimp in this li'l game.'

When Medway had finished explaining his plan, Shorty sat back and said mildly, 'Better fer you if I shoot you now, Jim. It won't hurt much and,' he added meaningfully, 'it'll be quick. Which is more than any o' us can expect if we get caught.'

81

'So we don't get caught!' his short friend snapped. 'Supposin' that black-dressed sonovabitch don't act like you say?' he asked.

Medway shrugged. 'He ain't the kind to check,' the Ranger stated.

'What sort o' diversion you plannin'?' Shorty asked curiously.

'Oh,' Medway shrugged. 'I thought I might borrow that purty yeller pony.'

CHAPTER TEN

Clarence Wilson's planning was certainly painstaking and meticulous, even Medway was forced to grudgingly admit that. Slim and Shorty had slipped away again in the early evening, leaving Medway to his own scheme and he'd woken next morning, to find the ranch transformed by the addition of flowers and bunting, half-a-dozen good horses in the corral, clearly reserved for presents and an appetizing smell of roast meat wafting from the kitchens.

He commented on this to Doc, when he encountered him later that day. The killer shrugged. 'They're like children,' he sneered, 'they want presents before they play.'

Medway nodded agreement. 'What's he feedin the bastards?' he asked with interest.

'Medina killed a couple of cows, I believe,' Doc sneered.

'Why?' Medway asked. 'I'd have thought livin' down here that fat greaser'd know better,' he explained. 'Apache'd sooner eat pony than cow and they like mule best of all. I allus found it on the sweet side myself,' he finished. Without giving the other a chance to speak, he went on, 'No hard feelin's about that business with the safe the other day, I hope,' he lied, holding out a hand. 'I just got mad seein' you an' that greaser playin' kid games.'

Ignoring Medway's hand, Doc said, 'I guess we're both in this for the dollars so let's just try and not get in each other's way.'

Medway shrugged in turn and fell in next to the other. 'By the way,' he asked, hoping he sounded sufficiently indifferent. 'Where you campin' the redskins?'

Doc waved vaguely towards the lake. 'Somewhere near the water,' he sneered. 'Mebbe it'll take away some of their damn stink.'

Vittorio, the Apache chief, and his men rode in a couple of hours before sundown. Medina greeted them ceremoniously, distributing presents and conducting the chief and his men to their allocated camping ground personally.

Medway tagged along surreptitiously and was close enough to the pair to hear Medina say, 'Soon there will be much food, much whiskey. Then tomorrow, you and your men will hear of the great plan to give back the land to the Apache!' That brought Medway up with a jerk. Apaches and greasers mixed like fire and gunpowder. They couldn't both have the land. Wondering how Wilson would work this one out, he headed towards his evening's entertainment.

Tonight, Medway treated the hacienda's citizens to another side of the character of the vicious gringo he had been playing. He got garrulously drunk.

'I's no goo' ol' fella,' he kindly informed the bartender, towards the end of his spree. 'Can' on'y drink outa one glass at a time.' Blankly, he stared at the bar, before assuming a beautiful smile and collapsing in a heap on the floor.

'This damn gringo, he is as heavy as a *caballo* an' he stink worse.' The Mexican holding Medway's shoulders sighed with relief as he pitched his end of the Ranger on to the dirty truckle bed. His companion gave a grunt of acknowledgement before leading the way out of the bare, dirty little room.

No sooner were the two Mexicans gone than Medway swung his legs soundlessly over the side of the bed and began pulling at his boots. Seconds later, with two blankets and his hat artistically arranged to simulate his sleeping figure and the room door locked, he swung over the window sill to be swallowed up by the warm velvet shadows.

Moving swiftly through the moonless darkness, he soon reached the front porch of the hacienda. Negas should still be at work in the kitchen and Medway pursed his lips doubtfully as he considered the role he wanted the boy to play.

'Kid's sure got nerve but still . . .' he muttered doubtfully, as he prepared to slip round to the rear of the building.

Suddenly, the front door was jerked open, flooding the veranda with light and Medway leapt soundlessly for the welcome darkness of the house's side wall. Heart pounding and expecting discovery at any moment, he heard a man and a woman, voices raised in argument, walking along the porch in his direction.

Next moment, a shapely, red-satin covered rump perched on the veranda rail and Marcia Hernandez said sharply, 'You know even for a gringo you're pretty stupid!'

Before her companion could reply, she went on, 'But you know what annoys me most is you think I am also that stupid.'

'If I don't think you're stupid, *querida*,' her companion said coaxingly, and shock bit into Medway as he recognized the voice of Lance Drago, 'I just ain't sure this game Wilson's playin' is such an all fired certainty.'

'That is because you do not understand the game he is playing,' the girl sneered. 'Listen,' she began, 'you think he would go to so much trouble for a measly hundred thousand dollars? No, *mi amigo*,' she said, 'he intends to own the whole of Texas, Arizona and New Mexico, with most of Southern California thrown in before he is finished!'

'You must be as mad as he is!' Drago sneered, and Medway sensed rather than saw the girl's impatient head shake.

'No,' she said softly. 'After Vittorio and Tortuga's men have raped and burned and killed across the South-west, there will be nothing left. There will be much good land, mines, towns, banks even, all needing money to start again. But with Vittorio and Tortuga and the others loose, who would be stupid enough to loan money to such people? But—'

'But if you knew, knew for certain that is,' Drago interrupted, 'that Vittorio and the rest weren't gonna be a problem ... why you could buy up banks, ranches, hell, all of it, for a song and then be sittin' pat!'

'Christ,' Drago went on, voice shaking, 'the ol' bastard'll make millions.'

'He says about a hundred million dollars over about ten years,' the girl said quietly. 'And if you listen to me and do what I tell you, we could help him spend it.'

There was a rustle and Medway saw a shirt-clad arm encircle the girl's waist.

'Oh don't,' she moaned softly,' not now.'

But there was no insistence in her voice and Medway was about to turn away, when Drago's voice purred, 'Only one thing, *querida*: how does he plan to get rid of the redskins and the greasers?'

'Doc has men at the mine, and guns. Don't talk now,' she finished imperiously, as Medway, with a satisfied grin, slipped off in search of Negas. Plainly, now, it all fitted and the Ranger shook his head in admiration at the other's ingenuity. Following the carnage and systematically robbing the banks, which he then intended to buy back for peanuts with their own money, was a work of genius. Medway's mouth tightened. After tonight's expedition, Mr Smartass Wilson might find there was a crimp in his little game.

Travis, the giant Negro who was Orsino Tortuga's right-hand man, bodyguard and pimp, had been enjoying himself. He'd pleasured himself to exhaustion with those three little *chi-chis* and now all he needed was a drink before he bedded down as usual beside Tortuga's pet stallion. Maybe he could persuade one of those little girls to keep him company, but first, he wanted whiskey and, as if in answer to his prayer, he caught sight of a young Mexican, carrying a large basket from which came an encouraging clink.

'Hey, boy, what you got there?' Travis rumbled and Jose Negas swallowed hard and tried to sound matter-of-fact as he answered.

'*Hola, señor,* I am taking some more whiskey to those pigs of Apaches.'

Travis shook his head. 'No you ain't, boy,' he corrected, grabbing Negas' arm in one giant hand as he reached into the basket with the other. Rummaging for a moment, he gave a rumble of disgust as he drew out an unlabelled bottle, filled with a pale, oily liquid.

Flinging the fire water away from him, he grasped Negas by his shirt front and said menacingly, 'Ain't you got nothin' in there fit for a gennleman to drink?'

'P-p-perhaps, *señor,*' Negas quavered, hardly having to fake his fear. 'Right at the bottom.'

With a grunt of exasperation, the Negro thrust the boy away and began to tear at the sides of the fragile basket. A moment later, his exertions were rewarded, as he reverently lifted a dark-brown bottle completely encircled by a green and black label.

'Ol Massa drink this,' he said to no one in particular. 'I gets my first drink of it right after I strangle the ol' bastard.'

Still muttering, the giant shuffled off in to the darkness in the direction of the stable where he and Tortuga had left their mounts.

Negas joined Medway at the rear of this building, just as Travis finished dismissing the guards already on duty there. Pulling the boy close, Medway breathed in his ear, 'Did he get the right bottle?'

'Couldn't keep it away from him,' Negas answered, and Medway responded with a short nod.

'We'll give him a while. Laudanum works quick but he's a big boy and I may have figgered the dose wrong.'

Medway needn't have worried. Before the pair had even managed to settle themselves comfortably with their backs to the sun-warmed adobe, the sound of stentorian snores greeted their ears.

Cautiously, Medway peered around the corner of the door frame, then he relaxed and got quickly to his feet, beckoning to his companion as he did so.

Nervously, the boy placed a hand on the rickety frame, clearly ready to bolt as he looked past the Ranger gingerly to where Travis lay slumped on his back in the clean straw, snoring volcanically.

'Aiee . . .' Negas whispered, flicking his hand from the wrist in the ancient Mexican gesture of disbelief. 'Is he human, that one?'

'Barely, I should say,' Medway offered judiciously. 'Here, help me with the pretty yeller pony. And keep that,' he finished, pointing at the gleaming belt and pistol that the boy was wearing, 'in its holster. I'll take care of any killin'!'

Tortuga's stallion proved highly strung but tractable and he offered no objection as the Ranger deftly saddled and bridled him. Medway glanced down at his companion's moccasin-clad feet then back to his own similar footwear before saying, 'Get out front and leave a few footprints. I'll bring him along.'

Negas drifted swiftly out of the door and Medway was about to lead the palomino after him when he caught sight of the Negro's mount in the adjacent stall. No Apache would leave a horse like that and Medway frowned doubtfully before tying off the yellow stallion and swiftly saddling the sorrel. He was about to lead both animals through the rickety doorway when Negas' voice said nervously, '*S-s-señor.* I..I..I thin' you better come out here!'

With sinking heart, Medway edged into the door frame to find Orsino Tortuga standing in the cleared space in front of the little adobe.

Outlined against the moonlight, he clearly wasn't alone. One sinewy arm was clamped around Negas' neck, the boy's body shielding him, while Tortuga's fancy Colt pressed into his side, in exactly the place where a bullet would do most good.

Medway jerked back as the Colt lifted and a voice said, in lisping Spanish, 'You better come out, gringo. And bring Rafael with you. He gets nervous around strangers.'

CHAPTER ELEVEN

Medway's glance swept round the stable, agile mind checking alternatives. One thing was sure, as soon as he put his nose out of the door, the greaser was set to blow it off. Unless . . .

Swiftly, he secured the sorrel, then turned to the big palomino. It was a bad idea at best, and his luck had been all bad, as usual, but he was out of choices.

'I'm comin' out,' he called, as he swung into the saddle, hands working rapidly. 'I ain't got no guns so don't shoot.'

In the dusty square, Tortuga grinned spitefully and tightened his grip on the boy. 'Come ahead, gringo,' he called, easing back the Colt's hammer, so that his voice covered the faint click. 'I give you my word you won' be hurt.'

As the head of the big palomino cleared the doorway, Tortuga levelled his Colt, intending to kill the gringo as soon as he emerged. But the stallion was alone and, as Tortuga indecisively lifted his weapon and scanned the shadows, Medway's voice snapped,

'Drop it, greaser! An' keep your mouth shut if you know what's good for you.'

'No, *señor*,' Tortuga returned, shifting his grip on the boy, 'I thin' it is you who should drop your pistol before this lettle one is verra dead.'

But shifting his grip proved Tortuga's undoing. Without warning, Negas jerked forwards and sank his teeth into the bandido's hand. Unable to control his instinctive response, Tortuga jerked his hand up, slapping the youth away.

Instantly, two shots smashed out of the darkness, sounding so close together they might have been one. Tortuga slumped, clawing at the holes in his chest, while his unfired pistol fell into the dust.

For a moment, everything was still, then Medway was unhooking his knee from the pommel of the palomino's saddle and sliding easily to the ground.

'Get his gun, kid, and make sure the bastard's cashed,' the Ranger ordered, dropping the reins of his borrowed mount and moving swiftly into the stable. Almost instantly, he was back with Travis's sorrel and, grabbing the reins of his victim's stallion, he swung aboard and tied the reins of Travis's mount to the dinner-plate horn.

'This one, he is finished,' Negas assured him, as the Ranger settled himself. 'The bullets, they were that close,' the young man went on enthusiastically, holding his palm up. 'In moonlight too!'

Medway looked down at the youthful, shining face and grimaced. 'Any fool can die in the dirt with a gun in his hand, like that one,' he snapped, more sharply than he meant, 'it's livin' that you gotta work at.' Yeah, livin', came the unbidden thought, and Jenny and little Bub.

Abruptly, Medway's face cleared.

'You got that pistol?' he demanded, and when the youngster nodded, he said, more gently, 'Check you got cartridges to fit it and then keep both them pistols hid. Now scat and make sure someone sees you real soon so they won't get suspicious.' Abruptly, he raised his head, and Negas heard his swiftly spoken warning.

'Git! They're comin'.' Then he was alone and the swift drumming of hoofs was diminishing into the night.

Medway found himself a seat on the wide veranda of the little *cantina* early the next morning and waited for the fun. It wasn't long in coming.

He was halfway through his first smoke of the day when he saw Travis, the Negro, striding towards the hacienda, accompanied by what looked like most of his men. The giant burst through the carved wooden doors and, almost immediately, Medway heard the sweet sound of argument.

But Wilson was no new chum when it came to manipulating people he wanted to use. Gradually, the sound of voices died away and then a Mexican, whom Medway didn't know, walked quickly out of the door, collected a horse and galloped swiftly in the direction of the Apache camp. Medway nodded in grudging admiration, struck once again by Wilson shrewdness. Who better than the Apache to track a horse-thief? Just as long as the kid had remembered to cover his tracks.

Later that morning, Medina called a council attended by the leaders of his little army.

Briefly, and to Medway's practised ear, clearly saying what Wilson had told him, he outlined the plan: rape, murder, an easy killing spree.

'And when we have killed all the gringos,' Medina added, 'the Apache will have their land and for the rest of us . . . more gold than you can count. Well, *amigos*,' the big man finished, 'who is with me?'

'Well, I for one, ain't!' Travis thundered, slamming a giant fist on to a nearby table top, 'You can't trust them red bastards! I still think they killed Orsino and took m' horse an' until you prove different, I ain't movin'.' He sat back and folded his arms with an air of finality which would have flustered a lesser man than Medina.

But the Mexican was playing for more money than he'd ever dreamed of and, more than that, he was backed by a master planner. So he smiled and said, 'I was jus' gettin' to that, *amigo*. Vittorio sent a couple of his boys to look around the stable and they come back with . . . this.' At his last word, two of his men appeared through the curtain-hung doorway that Medway had seen on his last visit, dragging between them the battered figure of Jose Negas.

Stumbling between his two captors, the youngster was led to the centre of the room before being savagely hurled to the floor. He looked up through a rapidly closing eye, as Medina leaned forward and said softy. 'Now, *amigo*, soon, for you, there will be much pain.' He jerked his head towards the grinning Vittorio, and from his position against the wall,

Medway saw consternation cross the youngster's face. Then his mouth tightened and he mumbled through bloody lips, 'You are a pig and the son of a whore who went with donkeys . . .' He continued in this vein for nearly a minute, with Medina's face growing redder and more coarsely veined, while Vittorio and his Apaches bellowed their laughter.

When Negas finally stopped from a combination of breathlessness and failure of invention, the big Mexican stood, hands clenching and unclenching, speechless with rage, before screaming, 'String him up by the feet and then bring fire and a sharp knife! Soon he will be glad to tell all he knows!'

'Don't waste your time, you fat greaser bastard,' said a soft, drawling Texas voice and heads turned in the direction of the speaker as Medway moved catlike across the room towards the big hacienda owner.

'He can't tell you nothin',' Medway went on, hands hanging easily over his Colts. 'I stole them ponies and turned 'em loose in the redskins' remuda. And I killed that cow turd Tortuga,' he snapped, twisting to keep Travis in view as the big Negro lurched to his feet. 'I done it all and I made him,' the Ranger finished, pointing at the prone Negas, 'help me.'

For endless seconds of unbearable tension the situation hung in the balance, then Medina shrugged and said savagely, 'But why? You are here for the money like the rest of us? Why would you do this?'

Medway grinned savagely. 'I hate greasers like poison and Apaches are wuss.' He shrugged. 'I thought it'd be funny to see 'em fightin' each other.'

It almost worked. Then Doc shook his head and his

hands lifted to hover over his gun butts.

'No,' he said softly, 'I don't believe it. Drop your belt. You can be our guest until the boss' – here an almost imperceptible headshake towards the door – 'decides how much use you still might be.'

Medway shook his head and folded his arms across his chest.

'I ain't leavin' my guns,' he stated flatly, his exaggerated head jerk becoming an insulting parody, 'till the boss tells me to. And I ain't doin' nothin' you or that fat greaser pimp might have in mind.'

Goaded almost to madness by Negas' insults, this final provocation proved too much for Medina. With a bull-like roar, he leapt towards the lean, two-gun man who had goaded and ridden him. Too late, Doc yelled a warning as, covered by the big man's torso, Medway went for his guns in a flickering blur of speed.

His first shot smashed into Vittorio's chest, hurling the Apache back against the wall. His second came within a whisker of ending Doc's career and a third drove into Medina's thigh as the big man scurried for cover and Drago stepped from the shelter of the crowd and slashed a gun into the side of Medway's head.

Desperately, the Ranger twisted, trying for a shot at his assailant but the barrel hammered in again and Medway dropped like a stone.

'God damn that gringo bastard,' Medina swore shakily, while being helped to his feet. 'Give me a gun: I swear I kill him now.'

'No.' Doc's voice was flat, lost to all emotion. 'Search him and I mean everything, Pedro,' he said to a little wizened desperado at his side. 'Then bring his things to me.' He eyed Drago speculatively. 'I have a feeling our Mr Medway may not be quite who we think he is.'

'Christ, how in hell did I know he was a Ranger?' Drago whined desperately.

The outlaw stood in front of Wilson's desk. Behind it, the crippled banker toyed with Medway's battered star in circle badge, while Doc and a heavily bandaged Medina looked on. Drago was weaponless and three heavily armed guards stood in a loose semi-circle behind him.

'See, here's my problem,' Wilson began, without looking up and as though Drago had never interrupted him. 'You set the Wayside job up and it was sweet. Nothing could go wrong, but it did and then, you turn up here, broke, and with this so-called safe-blower tagging along. Now, someone spoilt your plan and if it was this Ranger and he's been trailing you ever since, it all makes sense. Especially if you thought you'd shaken him, then found you'd led him straight to us. And there's nothing else that fits quite so neatly.' He paused, before leaning forward and adding in a savage whisper, 'What do you think?'

'I-I-I . . .' Drago stammered.

'Just like I thought,' Wilson interrupted savagely. 'Throw him in with the Ranger while I decide what to do with them.'

Left alone with his son and Medina, Wilson steepled his fingers and eased back in his chair.

'So where are we?' he asked, of no one in particular. 'Tortuga dead, Vittorio dead. Can we still make it work?' he demanded, keen glance sweeping over Medina.

'Tortuga's men will follow Travis,' Medina said confidently, 'He may be better for us; tha' Orsino, he was one sneaky son of a bitch. *Que malo*—'

'So the greasers'll play,' Doc interrupted. 'What about the redskins?'

'Mebbe, mebbe not,' Medina admitted uneasily. 'They think Vittorio's medicine went bad because Medway killed him and that makes them think they'll end up the same way.'

Wilson thought briefly then said to his son, 'Get the guns here by morning, day after tomorrow.' With a glare at Medina he demanded, 'Suppose they saw the man who killed their chief destroyed by another man? That would mean the other man's medicine was more powerful, wouldn't it?'

'Sure,' Medina shrugged. 'But how . . .' he began. Then, he saw the beginnings of Doc's self-satisfied smile and Wilson's sneering glance at his son.

CHAPTER TWELVE

It came as something of a shock for Medway, when he opened his eyes and found Lance Drago glaring down at him.

Head spinning and sick and dizzy as he was, he couldn't do much except glare back. The dizziness passed and with its going speech returned.

'You down here for more fun and games?' Medway rasped.

'No,' Drago admitted, with a tight grin. 'You and me are caught in the same loop, although I got an idea I may be loose before long.'

'Yeah?' Medway demanded without much interest. The pain in his head had localized and subsided to a dull ache across his temples and he was able to take a look at his surroundings. It wasn't very encouraging.

They'd been locked into what looked like an adobe forage store. It had no windows and the only passage for light and air was through the cracks between the massive door and its ill-fitting frame.

Seeing the direction of Medway's glance, Drago sneered, 'Don't bother even thinking about it. That door's two inches thick and there's two guards. Even if you killed them both, they ain't got the key. Gal brings it with her from the kitchen every time she fetches food an' stuff.'

'Thinks of everything, don't he?' Medway said, gingerly feeling the lump on his head then wishing he hadn't. 'He's pretty smart, you gotta give the ol' bastard that,' he finished thoughtfully.

'Give him a goddam bullet in the back o' the head, that's what I'd like to give him!' Drago snapped.

That night and another day and a night passed quietly and after a breakfast of the everlasting frijoles and tortillas, Medway was just beginning to regret the loss of his smokes when the door slammed open to reveal a grinning Doc framed in the entrance.

Without preamble he said, 'Drago, for some reason known only to himself, the boss still thinks you may be useful, so you can get out. But understand this,' he went on, as the outlaw made to pass him, 'it's only a reprieve. Your next mistake will be your last. I personally guarantee it.'

'On your feet, Ranger,' he continued, with an anything but reassuring grin, as a white-faced Drago pushed by him into the fierce sunlight. 'We're putting on a little show for the red sticks and guess who's the main attraction!'

Swiftly, Medway's hands were tied behind him and he was half led, half dragged to the little horse corral where he'd seen the last man executed. Doc shoved unceremoniously through the crush of spectators and ducked under the crowded rails, motioning for

Medway to be pushed through after him.

Without ceremony, the Ranger was shoved to the centre of the open space, his bonds were cut and he was left to stand, rubbing at his wrists while Doc collected a cloth-covered object from where it leant against the rails, before turning to face his audience.

He lifted the object, still in its cloth wrapping and silence gradually descended. When he could make himself heard, Doc began in fluid Spanish, 'Our friends, the Apache, came to us led by the great war chief Vittorio.' There were mutterings around the circle because, amongst the Apache, a dead man's name is never used and he is only referred to obliquely. Doc must have remembered this because he grimaced and went on. 'The one who is gone was a great chief but his medicine was bad. Now, comes a new chief.' He gestured at a squat and phenomenally ugly Indian standing outside the corral rails. 'To show that his medicine is good he brings these.' Doc jerked the wrapping from the object in his hand, to reveal a gleaming Winchester repeater.

'With these,' he went on, 'you will sweep the white man before you. Who will be first to try? Will you, Satanhya?' he said, gesturing towards the new Apache chief.

Without a word, the Indian ducked lithely into the corral and held out his hand. Doc swiftly shoved cartridges into the loading gate of the repeater, worked the action and handed the weapon to Satanhya.

'And just to show any who doubt that the white man who killed V—— the other one has lost his medicine,

101

why don't you try it on the Ranger?' Doc offered spite-fully, as Satanhya lovingly fondled the weapon.

Grinning wickedly, the Indian raised the rifle to his shoulder but before he could fire, Medway, who had been gazing absently into the crowd, intoned, in a clear, cold voice, 'Beware. Satanhya. Rangers' magic is very powerful!'

Turning to the crowd, Medway raised his arms and shouted, 'Do any here remember the fight the Rangers made at Indian Wells? Or Casa Grande? Who rode home that day?' Amid an increasing muttering, he faced Satanhya again.

'Only Rangers rode home that day and the Apache lay in the dust. It was because the Rangers have big medicine and cannot be killed.' Medway finished, folding his arms across his chest.

Unbelievably, it almost worked. Satanhya hesitated, allowing the rifle to drop from his shoulder, until Doc snapped, 'Are you an Apache or a child to be fright-ened of stories?' he demanded. 'For Chris'sake, shoot the loud mouthed bastard!' he added in English.

Abruptly, Satanhya's mouth tightened; he slapped the rifle to his shoulder, aimed carefully and squeezed the trigger. There was a loud crack, quite unlike the normal report of a Winchester and Satanhya screamed and clapped both hands to his face. Doc leapt towards the Indian only to skid to a halt as he caught a glimpse of the rifle which the Apache had thrown aside in his agony. Its barrel had split like a banana clear to the receiver but there had still been enough residual energy to hurl the breech block into Satanhya's face. What had happened was plain enough and seeing the cold smile on Medway's face was all the confirmation Doc needed.

Abruptly, he jerked up and started towards the Ranger only to be interrupted by a guttural Apache voice and Medina whining urgently, 'Doc, it's the shaman! He says the gods are angry and there can be no more fighting until both chiefs are buried. Jesus Maria, Doc, they're leaving!'

'Looks like you bin out-played, Doc,' Medway offered waspishly. 'What you gonna do now?' As if in answer, the black-dressed killer threw up his arms.

'Wait! Wait, all of you! It was a trick! Georges, check the rest of those rifles! Wait, goddamn it, he isn't a magician.' As one or two of the Indians looked back, Doc went on, 'He's a man. And I'll prove it because I'm gonna kill him now.'

One or two of the Apache exchanged glances. If the white man could be killed, then his medicine wasn't as strong as he claimed and the war path was still open to them.

Finally, one white-haired brave shrugged and said in limping Spanish, ' Show us then. Kill him, now.'

'My pleasure,' Doc snapped, jerking on his gloves and flicking out his weighted quirt to clear the lash.

Medway crouched, waiting as Doc moved in, following his quirt hand. They circled, watchful, then suddenly the quirt slashed in, driving at Medway's face.

But, unbelievably, the Ranger wasn't there and, instead, Doc felt his arm gripped and wrenched up his back. Arm and hand were burning like fire as the quirt was wrenched from his grip just as he managed to tear himself loose. He twisted, hands raised to ward off the expected blow, but it never came, because instead of using the quirt, Medway calmly tucked it into the back strap of his jeans and, raising his fists, advanced on his assailant.

'Figure that makes us about even, Doc,' Medway offered, as he feinted and smashed a lightning right into the other's face.

Stung to madness, Doc slashed at Medway with a clumsy backhand and the Ranger raised a negligent hand to push it aside. His hand contacted momentarily with the back of the other's leather glove and he had just time to see the look of triumph cross Doc's face before his hand and forearm were enveloped in a fiery pain the like of which he had never known.

Through the veil of tears which had sprung unbidden to his eyes, he saw Doc raise his fist for a second blow and he backed desperately, barely avoiding the other's clumsy downswing. If anything, the pain was increasing with each passing second and, even worse, it was accompanied by a numbing paralysis that seemed to be heading for the shoulder.

Medway risked a look behind him. Within feet, there was a worn snubbing post and, as Medway dodged Doc's clumsy rush and nursed his injured arm, the beginnings of a desperate plan began to form.

Awkwardly, the Ranger manoeuvred until his back was to the post and he was able to grip the worn timber with his good arm. He would need to be quick because, even as he gripped the post, a wave of dizziness and nausea swept over him so strongly that he almost fell. Seeing Medway stagger, Doc laughed.

'Liking it, Ranger?' he crowed. 'It's a little something Dad picked up in China. It wears off after a few hours unfortunately, but that isn't going to be soon enough for you!' At the last word, Doc leapt forwards, fist raised to strike.

Over-confidence proved his undoing, however, because somehow Medway ducked the blow and using the post for support, drove his foot squarely into his tormentor's stomach. Doc gave a hiccuping gasp and bent forwards, only to meet a smashing blow from Medway's good arm coming the other way. Doc dropped like a stone, and Medway slumped beside him, scarcely better off than his victim. His world had just begun to slip into darkness when he heard a rasping Mexican voice say, 'What shall we do with them, *señor?*'

'Take Doc to the house,' Medina's voice said, then paused, before adding, 'Put the gringo back in the store. We'll let Travis think up something real special for him!'

Night had fallen with its customary Border quickness and Medway found himself waking, yet again, to a headache and imprisonment.

'Christ,' he muttered softly, when his head seemed almost to have returned to its normal size, 'whatever that bastard was using sure packed a wallop.'

Outside the door of the forage store, where his captors had returned him, there was a sudden dry scrape and a muffled groan, and, wincing at the effort. Medway picked up his hat and centred it carefully on

105

his head. It was about time those two showed up. Medway had been expecting them since Slim had signalled him from the corral rails that morning.

'Jim, Jim,' a familiar voice hissed urgently.

Medway sat up, fighting the upwelling nausea and hissed back. 'Unless you figure to bust down that door, Shorty, you'll have to get the key from the kitchen.'

There was a pause and then Slims' voice said, 'And just how you figure we should do that! We gotta get you outa there, Jim,' the little man went on anxiously, 'the Indians are set to up stakes but that Travis looks to be arranging some mighty original entertainment for you come sun-up.'

For a second, Medway racked his brains, then he said, 'Try the kid. He works in the kitchen and mebbe he knows where to get the key.'

Silent as death, Slim and Shorty slipped through the gathering shadows to fetch up at the little stock corral which faced the double door to the kitchen. Carefully, a hatless Slim scanned the opening before ducking down and whispering, 'There's only one kid and from the way Jim told it last time, it's gotta be him. Only thing is, he's on the other side, by the stove, and ain't no way to reach him without going through the place.'

For a moment, Slim watched his tall companion, only to suddenly see a grin replace the habitual frown of concentration which always accompanied any intense mental activity on Shorty's part.

'I've figgered 'er out, Slim,' the tall one assured his irascible companion. 'You remember that time down south when Lippy Joe figgered he had me holed up and hogtied? 'Member how you got me out?'

For a moment, puzzlement replaced temper on the little man's face, to be followed a split second later by returning memory. His memories were not of the pleasantest kind to judge by his words.

'Yeah, I remember,' Slim hissed as loud as he dared. 'I remember it was dark and I still had to knife that big callabozo who rode for Joe. Not to mention Joe and his bed boy when they figgered to—'

'That was just one o' them things,' Shorty assured his friend. 'I'll get you the stuff.' And the tall one was gone before Slim could begin to voice his objection.

CHAPTER THIRTEEN

It had been a perplexing, frightening day for Jose Negas. He'd seen the slow spoken Texan who'd befriended him about to be executed in the corral and had been set to try and shoot the Apache himself, when the man's rifle magically exploded. Then Doc had had his turn and been beaten.

Now, the man people said was a Texas Ranger was penned up and, with daylight, he was going to be executed in the most nauseating way, without any chance of defending himself. And as if he didn't have enough trouble, this smelly, ragged old woman was pushing her way past him to get to the table.

'*Mamasita*,' Negas began politely, then stopped as an unmistakably male Texas voice rasped, '*Estas* Negas, Jose Negas?' it demanded. For a moment, Negas was stunned, then good sense reasserted itself and he jerked his head towards a doorway that plainly led deeper into the building.

Once hidden from prying eyes, Slim wasted no time. He flipped back the filthy shawl that he had used as a head covering and spat rapidly in Spanish, 'No

108

time to talk, kid, just listen. Jim's in a tight spot and since he says you're a friend, we need your help.'

'Sure,' the boy nodded instantly. 'Anything,'

'Good.' Slim took his hand from the wicked Toledo dagger that was his only weapon and said, 'The key to the place where he's caught is in here somewhere. We gotta have it and fast!'

'*Sí*,' Negas nodded again. 'I know where it is, I will get it and come quick to the prison.' He stood back and regarded the short, ugly old Texan, before shaking his head. 'You better be careful, *amigo*, a pretty girl like you could get in trouble here.'

'Thanks,' Slim growled, 'I'll try and remember it.'

It's debatable whether Slim remembered it or not but it is a fact that he'd all but reached the door of the kitchen when he found his way bared by a giant, scar-faced *bandido* who appeared to have been recently dipped in a mixture the main components of which consisted of tobacco, horse piss and rot-gut whiskey mixed in about equal quantities.

Shorty recoiled involuntarily and the Mexican laughed and grabbed the little man's arm, yanking it out of the stinking rags that covered it.

For a second, he glared down at a wrist which was suddenly as thick and hairy as his own. For just one vital split second, he was unable to make the connection between brain and voice and in that instant, Slim acted. His knee drove upwards, catching the man cleanly between the legs and a rapid snatch closed his mouth, as in the same movement, Slim propelled him through the door and into the darkened yard.

Unfortunately, the massive shove caused Slim to over balance and he found himself knocked sprawling while his assailant landed feet away from him in the dust of the horse road. Instantly, the little man regained his feet and lunged at his opponent, knife in hand, but the other had also been trained in the ruthless school of border warfare and the instant Slim needed to close the gap between them was time enough for him to open his mouth to emit the single yell that would ruin the whole night's proceedings.

But opening his mouth was as far as he got because even as Slim threw himself desperately across the intervening space, a tall, thin shadow appeared behind the *bandido*, a hand clamped across his open mouth and silver flickered momentarily at the man's throat. The tall, fat figure stiffened momentarily then slumped to the ground as Shorty released his hold and wiped his giant Bowie knife clean on the Mexican's filthy charro jacket.

'What in hell kept you?' Slim hissed, as he divested himself rapidly of his filthy disguise.

'Stealin' hosses,' came the laconic reply. Despite himself, Slim asked, 'Anything good?' There was a chuckle from where Shorty was hoisting the body of his victim across one broad shoulder before setting off into the darkness.

'I took that purty yaller pony Jim's so fond of. Figgered you an' me oughta' git somethin' outa this damn business.'

Slim nodded to himself. A Palomino stud would make a real nice addition to the ranch's breeding stock. If they and the stallion ever reached home alive, that is.

It didn't take the two oldsters many minutes to dispose of the body, but it had still been too long for Jose Negas whom they found waiting with the newly released Medway outside the fodder store.

'So what now?' Medway demanded. 'Guns and hosses would sure sound good.'

Diffidently, Shorty cleared his throat. 'Took care of,' he said gently. 'Our ponies are waitin' up on the rim rock and I got us a spare apiece in the brush there and them wore-out relics you use instead of decent guns are on your saddle, Jim.'

'Then what we waitin' for?' demanded the ever patient Slim.

At first, everything proceeded smoothly. They collected the ponies without incident, checked the gear, Medway sighing with relief at feeling the familiar weight of his belts tugging at his hips. Without fuss, they mounted and walked the ponies up the first of the slopes that would take them out of the immediate area of the hacienda, when a raucous bellow split the night air.

'*Quien es?*' came the challenge and the only sound to follow was the soft slapping of old leather as Shorty eased his long barrelled 45:70 repeater from its sheath.

'Kin you see 'im, Slim?' the tall one whispered, peering up at the star-bright Mexican sky.

'Fer Chris'sake, put that away!' his bosom companion hissed viciously. 'One shot'll wake the whole camp.'

'*Quien es!*' This time the challenge was more peremptory and Medway, who was behind Negas, distinctly heard the sound of a Winchester's action being worked. Without any clear option, the Ranger's hand was straying to his Colt, although unwilling to risk the noise of a shot, when he heard Negas' voice, relaxed and drowsy, coming from somewhere in front of the leading horse.

'Eh, *amigo*, you wouldn't shoot me till I find my mule. My father, he will beat me sure if I get killed an' can't work tomorrow.' Abruptly, a figure topped with the usual sugar-loaf sombrero rose from behind a group of rocks barely twenty yards from the trail and moved towards the youngster.

'*Ai de mi,*' the man began, then he stiffened, staring wide-eyed and disbelieving at the handle of the Bowie knife which seemed to be growing from his chest, before folding silently to the ground.

'Good,' Slim began unnecessarily as Shorty slipped through the darkness. 'Git your sticker and . . .' He was interrupted by the winging snap of a shot ricocheting from a nearby rock as Shorty grabbed up his blade and vaulted astride his borrowed pony. Abruptly, the tall one jerked his mount around and there came a rifle's flat crack as Shorty snapped a shot at a figure silhouetted against the moonlight. The man jerked but stayed on his feet. Until, that is, Shorty's second bullet drove into his head and tumbled him to the ground.

'Christ, two o' the bastards. I'm gittin' old,' Shorty informed no one in particular as he fought his gun-shy pony. 'Let's git the hell outa here afore someone else starts shootin'.'

'Wait up,' Medway snapped abruptly. 'Keep them ponies still! Think about it. If'n you heard a coupla shots and then a herd o' ponies gallopin' away, what'd you do?'

'Head up here hell fer leather,' Slim snapped, 'which is what we should be doing away from here right now.'

'Suppose you heard a coupla shots, then . . . nothin'. What might you do then?' Medway went on remorselessly.

'I'd . . .' Slim began, then finished thoughtfully, 'I might do a lot o' things, but if'n I didn't hear no one runnin', I might even think it was just kids funnin'. I sure wouldn't come up here in no rush.'

'Right,' Medway confirmed. 'Git them ponies movin' . . . quietly.'

The 200 yards to the rim rock was probably the longest ride any of them had ever made. At any minute they expected to hear the hammering sound of hoofs breaking the stillness to tell them that their bluff had been called, but they reached the little hollow where Slim had hidden Cocoa and the other mounts without incident.

Medway eased himself in the saddle and looked down at the respectable remuda which occupied the bed ground.

'Just can't get rid o' them old habits, huh boys?' he demanded facetiously.

Shorty sniffed. 'If'n you look over there, Mr Smart Alec,' he said, clearly offended, 'you'll see why we need all these here pack horses.'

Medway did as he was told and after only a few seconds groping, he whistled and stood up.

'I guess these ain't had their barrels stuffed with sand an' blanket wool like the one Doc give the Injun,' he demanded, and before anyone could speak he continued, 'How many you got?'

Slim shrugged. 'Kid said about fifty peons at the mine, so we brung sixty to be on the safe side, just like you told us. We blocked the barrels of most of the rest—'

'Yeah,' Shorty interrupted, 'and just in case they found that, I pulled the breech pin outa a lot o' the others.' He nodded as he caught his partner's admiring chuckle. 'First time someone tries to fire one, it'll wreck the mechanism an' with any luck take the bastard's eye out!'

'You done good,' Medway decided, still rummaging, 'but this ain't a rifle,' he offered, poking an awkward blanket-wrapped shape.

'No, it ain't,' Slim admitted, 'but we figgered it might come in handy, if'n my nose is tellin' me true and that top soldier at the mine turns out to be straight.'

'Straight or not,' Medway said, swinging into his own saddle and turning Cocoa up the trail in the same movement, 'we can't just leave the kids' folks to it, I'm gonna powwow with the blue belly. You two bring the guns and don't forget the kid, 'cause we're gonna need him.'

Negas stared up the trail for a long time after Medway had gone. Then, as if returning to reality, he shook himself.

'Why would he do that?' he asked, of no one in particular. 'Why would he risk his life for a bunch of Mexicans?'

'It ain't so much that,' Shorty, who had overheard, informed him. 'An' it's a long story that we ain't got time fer now, but you can bite on this,' the tall one finished. 'If Jim Medway's your friend, he's your friend till the cartridges are gone and the Comanche are comin' over the walls.'

'You talk too much,' Slim snapped, 'but that is sure the plain truth. Get them guns packed and roped, we gotta be where we're goin' afore sun-up. An' you better hope,' he added as an afterthought, 'that I wasn't wrong about that top soldier.'

At that moment, some distance to the south-west, Sergeant Major Ike Malansky, the object of their speculations, was immersed in an entirely different problem.

As he explained to his old-time friend and side partner, Ernie Sinclair, cavalry regulations didn't cover it.

'I just ain't sure about that lieutenant,' he offered. 'It looks all right, except we got no written orders, nowhere we can draw supplies and we don't see that black-dressed sonofabitch for weeks at a time. These poor bastards are dyin' like flies and even the government wouldn't let that happen.'

'No,' Sinclair agreed, rubbing the bare patch on his regulation shirt, where the pattern left by the removal of a sergeant's hooks showed clearly. 'They wouldn't leave a bunch o' greasers to die. After all, they ain't enlisted men.'

115

Malansky sighed and changed the subject. 'Jus' don't feel right and I don't trust him.'

'He's an officer,' Sinclair offered succinctly, 'so that just goes without saying. Me for bed,' he finished. 'I'll check the posts before I turn in.'

Malansky nodded his thanks and eased a pair of enormous, cavalry-booted and spurred feet to the floor. Bed sounded good and Ernie would keep the men on their toes.

Dawn was just beginning to crowd daylight into the western sky, when some sixth sense which comes to old soldiers after too many dangerous trails, jerked Malansky awake. His hand was reaching for the butt of his old, long-barrelled Colt, when a soft double click warned him that whatever he was intending would probably find him way too late.

Moving slowly and carefully, he took his hand from under the pillow and reached for his pipe. There was a grunt of satisfaction from the other occupant of the room.

'Now that was real sensible,' Medway said softly, as Malansky fired up his old stink pot, 'And if you're sittin' real comfortable, Sergeant, I got a little story you may be interested to hear . . .'

CHAPTER FOURTEEN

'I goddamn well knew it,' Sinclair snapped, as soon as Malansky had explained the new situation to him. 'Goddamn officers!' he went on, Irish brogue twanging. 'Ain't one of 'em worth a bucket of horse shit!' Abruptly, he jerked his chin in Medway's direction. 'You figure he's OK, Ike?' and when Malansky nodded, Sinclair demanded, 'Why?'

'Because what he says makes sense. There was too much that stank about this set up from the start. I knew Lieutenant Wilson or Doc or whatever his goddamn real name is, was crooked, just couldn't prove it.' Malansky shrugged expressive shoulders. 'And by the time he'd got us here, there was no way home. Now there is. Besides,' he added ruefully, 'I kinda got a feelin' this here Ranger is straight.'

'Oh sure,' Sinclair offered, 'there's a way home all right, as long as we kin fight every Apache in the South-west.'

Medway shook his head. 'The Apache don't figger

in this.' Briefly, he described the incident at the hacienda and when he'd finished, Malansky nodded thoughtfully, while Sinclair gave a snort of laughter.

'You're sure a bearcat fer nerve, Ranger,' the latter offered admiringly, and Medway shrugged.

'Nothin' else to do,' he stated flatly, 'but you kin see that all we gotta worry about now is Tortuga's *bandidos*.'

'And how many you figger they might be?' Sinclair demanded. 'And in case you're wonderin' he went on, the Irish brogue lengthening again, 'our strength is fifteen, counting me and th' Polack.'

' 'Bout a hundred, but my partners are bringing a little surprise that'll help shorten them odds,' Medway explained. 'If they get here in time,' he added, with a glance at the rapidly paling sky.

Unfortunately, Slim and Shorty were late and some of Travis's *bandidos* knew a short cut. The first Malansky knew about it was when a bullet cut the air above his favourite head as he was making a brief inspection of the perimeter defences.

The sound of the bullet brought Medway at the run and he flopped down next to Malansky, breathing hard.

'What's happening?' the Ranger demanded and the sergeant shrugged expressively.

'They're shootin' at us and we can't shoot back 'cause anyone who looks over the top o' that ledge is gonna git his head blowed off,' the big man explained succinctly.

Medway thought swiftly then he said, 'Look, this

118

ain't no good. They got us pinned so we can't get my partners in nor the rest of us out. Come nightfall at the latest, they'll have most of the others here. Which means we can't wait for dark.'

Carefully, he scanned the surrounding camp, before asking, 'Is there a back way outa here that you and some of your boys could use with ropes?'

The big Pole shrugged, 'Sure, but—'

'Good,' Medway interrupted. 'So this is how we play it. . . .'

Hernando Lopez, brother of Marcia, was feeling pleased with himself. While Travis and Doc were wasting their time following Medway's tracks, Hernando had played a hunch and come straight to the mine. His tracker had found Cocoa's hoof prints in the pale of the dawn, confirming the Ranger's presence. Now, he was simply covering the only trail in or out and pot shooting at the soldiers to pass the time, knowing that he held all the cards.

He and his men were hidden in a tiny fold in the hills which gave perfect cover. He either hadn't noticed or had chosen to ignore the fact that one well-aimed volley would sweep the place from end to end.

As the sun climbed in the sky, however, Lopez was getting less fond of his little home from home and it was with something akin to relief that he saw a white flag waving above the defenders' rampart, indicating they wanted to parley.

Lopez settled himself comfortably and called, 'What you wan', gringo?'

'Figgered we might talk awhile,' Medway's voice

119

floated down, distracting Lopez from the small but significant sounds coming from his rear.

Involuntarily, the Mexican shrugged. 'About what should we talk, *señor*?' he asked spitefully. 'You are up there, we are down here. Pretty soon, me and my *amigos*, we will come and take what we want.'

'Perhaps what we should talk about then,' said a new voice, from somewhere behind Lopez' left ear, 'is how many of you boys'll be left alive if we open fire?' Gingerly, the big man turned his head to find himself looking into the bore of Malansky's cavalry pistol, while his men were covered by half-a-dozen grinning blue coats lining the rocks behind him. For a long second, Lopez glared into Malansky's blue eyes, then goaded to madness by something he saw there, he went for his pistol in a blur of speed. Malansky's order was lost in the crash of weapons and, as the smoke cleared, the big Pole glanced into the bloody, bullet-pocked little draw and shrugged.

'Whether it's cookin' or war,' he offered, to no one in particular, 'you sure don't want to keep all your eggs in one basket.' Carefully, he checked the horizon, then gestured with a big fist. 'Johnny, me lad,' he ordered, 'hide them bodies.' He paused listening, before adding, 'And unless I miss my guess, this'll be some friends Mr Medway's expectin'.'

'It sure all adds up now,' Malansky admitted, after Slim had shown him the new model Gatling gun. 'Lieutenant Wilson figgered to use us to finish off the Apache and *bandidos* once they'd been lured to this . . . this town with the God-awful name. You say it's a

120

good spot?' Malansky demanded of Slim.

'It's perfect,' the little man explained briefly. 'One central square, built inside an old adobe mission. Only three ways in, so three guns and no way out over the walls or anywhere else.'

'You gotta hand it to that ol' bastard Wilson,' Medway said. 'He uses the money he's been stealing from these peons to buy guns, which he then gives to the Apache and Tortuga, so they'll run wild through the South-west, which leaves him free to rob every bank in four states and use the money he's stolen to buy everything back for a song. And all with a nice shiny legal title attached.'

'And not only that,' Shorty finished, 'he uses the army to finish off the greasers and Indians, so it's not only watertight but it's legal as well. Hell, I wouldn't be surprised if'n them fools in Washington don' give him a medal!'

'You forgot the best part,' Slim added waspishly. 'We know what's gonna happen but you ain't got a scrap o' proof that'll stand up in a court o' law. So far all you could accuse him of is kidnappin' half a hundred greasers. And you can bet how worried a Yankee court'll be about that.'

Medway shook his head as he drew the worn Colt he carried on his right side. 'You're missin' the point, Slim,' he said, as he clicked open the loading gate and began to examine the cartridges. 'Big men have big enemies. You can't hide a game the size he's playin'. There'll be signs everywhere, signs the federal marshals'll spot easy as squat. He daren't leave any loose ends. Oh, there'll be rumours about what

121

happened here,' Medway went on, apparently satisfied with his inspection of the Colt, 'but as long as there's no one to point the finger and say "I seen it", rumours won't matter. Nope,' he went on, beginning a similar inspection of his left-hand pistol. 'It's him or us now. And he deserves to die and that's all.'

'You may find a hundred or so objections to that ridin' this way. Just in case you had forgot,' Shorty said mildly.

'I ain't forgot. You and Slim git that gun packed on a coupla ponies. Sergeant, mebbe you better pick yourself a coupla good men but not Mr Sinclair here. . . .'

'Might help if I knew what for,' Malansky offered reasonably.

'Just a little surprise party,' came the innocent reply. 'Fer about a hundred guests. By the way, is there any other way in apart from that trail in the ravine?'

Malansky thought a moment. 'Not 'less you want a two-day ride without water,' he began.

'Good,' Medway said abruptly. 'Now, here's what we do.'

'I don' like it,' Travis whined for the perhaps the tenth time in an hour. He looked up yet again at the lowering cliffs that lined their route. 'This place was made fer an ambush!'

'For the love of Christ and all his bastard saints,' Doc snapped, patience finally exhausted. 'Shut your whining mouth, or I'll shut it with lead. It's your goddamn fault we had to come this way.' Travis subsided into low mutterings and Doc turned his attention back to the trail.

It wouldn't have done to admit it to Travis, of course, but Doc found himself becoming increasingly concerned. The ravine they were following would not end for a good mile, and it had narrowed so much that it was all the party could do to ride two abreast. Doc glanced ahead, shading his eyes from the fierce early afternoon glare. And anyone who had that behind them would be impossible. . . . The thought was never finished, because, up on the rim rock, Malansky, having estimated the range to a nicety, dropped his hand and bellowed, '*Fire!*'

His men needed no second bidding and Doc, leading the group, found himself the subject of a murderous cross fire. He lost his hat, his horse and most of his right ear in the first thunderous exchange and Medway cursed as he jacked a round into the foul, smoking breech of his Winchester and snapped an ineffective shot at the black-dressed killer as Doc leapt behind the scanty cover offered by the body of his gelding.

Suddenly, the merciless coffee-grinder chatter of the Gatling gun stopped. Medway snatched a glance across as a cursing Malansky knocked out the first retaining bolts and tore the angular firing pin clear. Down below, the *bandidos*, scarcely believing their good fortune, were climbing aboard their horses and heading up the narrow ravine, oblivious to the fire poured down on them by the handful of men left to service the gun. Lead peppered the rocks around the Gatling and suddenly, disastrously, Malansky jerked in agony, before slumping into the dust. Medway only needed one look at the gaping head wound with its hideous exit hole, to know that the big Pole was beyond help.

'Leave him!' the Ranger snapped at the white-faced young soldier who was pulling the big man away from the gun. 'Leave him,' he repeated, more gently. 'He's cashed. Bust that gun, then get out.'

Stooping, Medway snatched up the firing pin from where it had fallen from Malansky's hand and shoving it into a pocket, turned up the slope to where his borrowed pony patiently waited. He didn't see the shot that tore through the young trooper he had ordered to wreck the Gatling gun, throwing him to the ground, and would probably have attached no importance to it if he had.

Medway and the rest of the detachment were well on their way back to the mine, pressed hard by a big group of bandidos, when Doc reached the remains of the gun.

Swiftly, he checked the weapon, then cursed, before his attention was attracted by a weak groan. It was the young soldier, barely alive. One of the *bandidos* reached for his knife, meaning to finish what the bullet had started, when Doc cursed him away and knelt beside the boy. He shook the young soldier ungently.

'Johnson, Johnson, it's me, Lieutenant Wilson. Where are you hit, son?' Doc went on larding his voice with an uncharacteristic concern. Abruptly, the boy's eyes jerked open and he gripped the black-clad arm supporting him.

'Sir,' the boy began, 'Sarge Mal . . . said you was a trai . . .'

'It was a trick, boy,' Doc assured him. 'It was Malansky who was crooked. Where's the firing pin for this gun?' he demanded brutally.

'They said . . . you . . . planned . . . a . . . massacre, millions . . . in . . . gold . . .' the dying boy went on, as his eyes clouded.

'Goddamn it, where's that pin?' Doc demanded, dropping his pretence of concern and giving the boy a violent shake.

'Ranger . . .' the young man began, then his body jerked spasmodically and his head lolled backwards. Without any further regard for his trooper, Doc dropped the body and stood up, face working.

'Everywhere I goddamn well look, that bastard's getting in the way and . . . you,' he stormed, pointing at an innocent looking Drago, 'you're the stupid sonofabitch who led him here . . .' He stopped because he found himself looking into the yawning bore of Drago's Colt.

'I don' like to be called that,' Drago said easily. 'You ever do it agin, I'll kill you. But for now we need each other. What exactly has Medway got that you need?'

'His life,' Doc stormed, completely out of control. 'I'll pay anyone a thousand dollars who can prove he's killed the bastard!'

Unbeknown to his admirers, just at that moment, five miles away, as Medway encouraged his tired pony up the sand and rock-rutted slope that led into the mine, one of Doc's men came near to earning that prize. His shot missed the Ranger, but it proved nearly as disastrous, because it passed six inches in front of his spurred and booted foot, slammed into the chest of his little mount and tore through the heart muscle, killing him instantly. Medway felt the spring go out of the gallant little beast and had just time to kick his feet from the stirrups and throw himself clear before his mount collapsed in a sprawling heap.

Stunned and shaken, Medway still heard the yell of triumph as the leading group of *bandidos*, who had been only a long rifle shot behind him, urged their own mounts forward in a desperate race, the prize for which was his death.

Seated yards from his dead pony and with his Winchester trapped in the saddle skirts, Medway dragged out his Colts, painfully aware that they contained only two shots apiece and prepared to sell his life as dearly as possible. One hundred yards from safety, came the thought unbidden, and it might have been a hundred miles. In the press of circumstances, he could be forgiven for not noticing that the firing pin of the new model Gatling gun had fallen from his pocket and was lying on the other side of his dead horse, in plain view of anyone looking up the slope.

CHAPTER FIFTEEN

Closer thundered the bandit horde and a few optimistic shots began to peck at the sand around the Ranger, when he heard, from up the slope, Slim screaming a warning.

'Jim, Jim!' the little man bellowed, 'Get down! Fer Chris'sake, *duck*!' Without understanding, but obedient to the partner he had come to trust, Medway threw himself sideways.

It wasn't a moment too soon.

As Medway's face ground into the dust a level, Irish voice, larded with all the bad temper one of Her Majesty's very own green-jacketed Rifleman could muster when things have turned bad and the range has dropped to a bare hundred yards, bellowed, 'Front rank, present.' A bare second passed, then, '*Fire*!' the same voice bellowed again.

A storm of lead flailed the air above Medway's head and, wisely, he didn't look up as the raucous voice called the drill which had saved the Widow's out-numbered and out-gunned regiments times beyond count, from the fever-strewn wastes above Delhi's gates to the mealie-bagged ramparts by the little ford in Zululand known as Rorke's Drift.

'Rear rank, present' – a pause – '*fire*! Move on! Reload that weapon, yez dozy bastard.' Another pause – 'Rear rank, present, *fire*!' A third volley, more ragged than the last, but by now, the *bandidos* had had enough.

They scattered, like wind-driven leaves, intent only on finding cover from the flailing hail of lead and the bellowing Irish voice.

'Yez better git yourself up, Yank.' The harsh Dublin accent grated in Medway's ear as he found himself gripped and jerked upwards to face Sinclair's brick-red features.

'Get the Ranger's rifle and fall back, quick,' the Irishman bellowed.

'Corporal,' he roared again, and amazingly a cotton-clad peon, handling his stolen rifle with all the familiarity of a veteran, snapped a brisk salute.

'None o' that now,' Sinclair ordered. 'Twelve men, two ranks, cover our backs!'

'*Sí*, the old man snapped and a staccato string of orders burst from his lips. Magically, the two ranks formed and the white-clad Mexicans beat a fighting retreat, covering the labouring Irishman as he lugged a half-conscious Medway through the makeshift barricade thrown across the entrance to the mine.

'Sure, a Dublin recruitin' sergeant'd be glad to offer any of these darlin' boys the Widder's shillin' to see 'em in the Rifle Green,' the Irishman offered, as he ushered the Mexicans through the hole in the barricade and dropped the wicket into place.

'*One!*' Sinclair sang abruptly as he snapped his Winchester to his shoulder and neatly drilled a bandit, who, at 200 yards, had been foolish enough to expose a two-inch area of his skull to the corporal's Rifle-trained eye. Twenty years before, Sinclair had undergone a three-month course of musketry which had given him a sore shoulder, a bruised and blackened thumb and the ability to hit a man-sized target at 600 yards nine times out of every ten. Being a member of Her Majesty's Rifle Regiment had ensured he received the benefit of almost constant practice.

Sinclair jacked another round into his weapon and squinted through the dispersing smoke as Medway shook his head and joined him.

'Don't think I ain't grateful,' the Ranger offered, 'but how in hell did you train farmers to be soldiers in half a day and where did that Irish accent come from? You was strictly American when I left.' Abruptly, there was an incoherent yell from down the barrier and a slow Texas voice bellowed, '*Two.*'

'He didn't need to train them boys,' said Slim's voice at his shoulder. 'I discovered that me n' Shorty and ol' Juan over there, had got a little something in common.' He indicated where the white-haired peon Sinclair had addressed as 'corporal' moved easily around the barricades passing a word of advice or a joke as he came to each man. Occasionally, one of the peons would look anxiously at Sinclair, still straining his eyes through the smoke, and there would be a few words in Spanish, a gesture and the men would resume their patient watching.

'What might that be?' Medway demanded, as he

snatched back his rifle and began to examine it.

Slim looked embarrassed and said in a small voice, 'Oh, we all rode for Juarez a time or two.' It took a minute to sink in.

'Juarez? *El Presidente*?' Medway demanded.

'Oh, well, it weren't like it sounds,' Slim explained. 'Ol' Benito was kinda hard pressed an' we jist ... helped him out. With a few guns. Turns out some o' these boys are ol' time Juaristas too. Now come away and don't distract the sergeant.'

'Why?' Medway demanded.

'On account of I'm bettin' ol' Juan that Sinclair'll pot more o' them *bandidos* than Slim gets. That stringbean's gittin' old an' I figger to make me some drinkin' money.' He indicated the anxious peons. 'Most o' the boys figger like me and are backin' the sergeant.'

For a moment, Medway was lost for words then he said softly, 'Don't fer Chris'sake let the future o' the Western United States git in the way o' your gamblin', will you?'

'Sure as hell not!' Slim agreed, before asking, ' Give you two to one against the stringbean if you're interested, Jim?'

Half an hour had passed before Medway noticed their assailants' interest in the body of his dead mount.

Sure glad I weren't ridin' Cocoa, he told himself, but I wonder why them greasers are so interested in that pony?

Suddenly, there was a flurry amongst the figures which were gathered in the undergrowth off the trail and well out of range. Medway snapped his old field-glasses to his eyes in time to see a black-dressed figure jump from the seat of a small buckboard. He also saw something else which sent him in search of Sinclair.

'Sergeant,' he began, as a lack of activity in front of the man's position drew his eye, 'did we lose anyone apart from Malansky at the ravine?'

'I ain't sure,' the Irishman admitted, New York accent firmly back in place.

'Sim,' he bellowed, and when a lean, fair-haired Texan looked up, Sinclair said, 'Call the roll. See who we've lost.'

Dusk had begun to fall when the soldier returned.

'All present and accounted fer,' he drawled, 'except Malansky and the kid.'

Medway nodded. 'That, at least, explains why the Gatling gun's still in one piece,' he stated. 'Sure as hell hope they didn't catch that kid alive.'

'I ain't tryin' to tell you your job, Ranger,' Sinclair began, 'but if that gun's still workin', we could be in for a hard time.' He pointed downwards. 'They only got to get into that fold o' ground and they can sweep the gate and enough o' the barricade on each side to make us hard to find. And a thing like that'd cut the gate to pieces in a coupla minutes. How you figger they's fixed for cartridges?'

'They got lots,' Slim interrupted, 'and,' he added significantly, 'me an' Shorty couldn't find no way to bust 'em. Leastways not till it was too late.'

'It shouldn't be a problem, the gun won't work without this,' Medway assured them, feeling in his pocket. His expression quickly changed as he method-

131

ically turned out his jeans.

'Damn,' the Ranger swore, 'I must have dropped it when they shot my horse.'

Ignoring the sporadic shots that nicked the wood-work around him, Medway risked a quick look over the barrier, jerking back as a near miss jerked his sombrero awry.

'Close,' he offered, investigating the hole with a finger.

'It wouldn't have mattered,' Slim offered waspishly. 'Gettin' hit in the head ain't somethin' *you* need to worry about. Did you see it?'

'Nope,' Medway admitted, slapping on his damaged headgear, 'but it don't matter. We either get us some help by tomorrow night, or we might as well give up. Our cartridges'll sure be gone by then.'

Sinclair nodded in confirmation. 'Where you figgerin' to raise help?' he asked.

'Paesar Querte,' came the surprising reply.

'You ain't gotta convince 'em of anything,' Medway repeated tiredly, for the fifth time. 'Just tell that deppity that the man who killed Buck De Grace is here and all they need to do is come get 'im. Oh, and find out what calibre o' weapon he was shot with,' he added, as an afterthought. 'It might save my neck.

Slim nodded half-heartedly. 'Sure hate to be the one to go,' he grumbled, 'seems like we're runnin' out on you fellas.'

'You two relics are the best men for the job,' Medway assured him. 'Once you get goin', none o' them greasers'll have a chance at catching you.'

'He's right, Slim,' Shorty offered, silently easing the barricade aside, 'Let's get at 'er. We ain't got much time if'n we want to be back by tomorrow with a posse.'

At first, everything went well. Moving silently through the accommodating sand, Shorty reached the far side of Medway's dead pony and after a few seconds work, slipped the angular firing pin into his belt. Several seconds passed as he patiently checked the night air for sight or sound or scent of the enemy.

Eventually satisfied, Shorty continued his journey down-slope, angling towards a large chaparral thorn which he knew sheltered the *bandido's* remuda.

Reaching the bush, Shorty rose to his full height, followed seconds later by his partner. Slim reached out a careful hand to part the screening branches, when he heard a familiar double-click and a sneering Mexican voice said, 'Light the torch, Sancho, and let us see the little birds that have come visiting our nest.' Twenty feet away, in the pitch darkness, Medway saw the flare of the torch and wriggled sideways desperately, hugging the uneven contours of the ground. Once clear of the torch's circle, he rose and sprinted noiselessly towards the main camp.

Fortunately for Slim and Shorty, the *bandido* who had captured them was a talker. As the torch flared, he walked slowly forward, brandishing a battered Colt, before saying, 'So you are leaving, *amigos*? 'Verra sensible, but you should have walked. Now,' he shrugged, 'you just got into trouble.' Slowly, savouring the moment, he raised his pistol until it was level with Shorty's forehead.

'*Vayas con D—*' he began, when suddenly from the camp behind there was a staccato burst of firing, followed by a screaming Comanche war cry. For a moment, the *bandido's* attention flicked up the slope and in that instant, Slim and Shorty burst in to action.

The revolver menacing the tall one's forehead was swept aside and, as the Mexican holding it turned back towards his intended victim, he met Shorty's giant Bowie knife coming the other way. Slim was a bare instant in front of his old-time friend, Colt leaping into his hand, apparently of its own volition, as his palm slapped back the hammer, emptying the pistol into the three remaining *bandidos* before any of them could think of lifting a weapon.

'Get the ponies,' Slim snapped, rapidly reloading, as Shortly dropped his victim and turned towards his friend, Bowie in hand.

The tall one nodded, then apparently remembering something, said anxiously, 'What about them Comanche, Slim?'

'That was Jim, you damn fool,' the little man snapped, then, seeing his partner's satisfied grin, returned it and said, 'Drinks are sure on me next time we hit town.'

'If we ever hit town, ' Shorty corrected, with his usual optimism, swinging aboard a restive pony and hooking his knee around the enormous pommel. In an instant, he disappeared down the other side and his voice, somewhat muffled by horse hide could be heard saying, 'Giddyap, you goddamn crowbait.' A pistol flashed and as one animal, the remuda turned down the slope away from the bandit camp.

*

About to slip through the barricade into the mine, Medway heard the herd's departure and turned to look after his friends. It was perhaps as well for his peace of mind that he didn't know that, in swinging aboard this restive pony, the firing pin of the Gatling gun had slipped from Shorty's belt and now lay in plain sight only feet away from the bodies of the boys' latest victims.

CHAPTER SIXTEEN

Which was where Doc found it next morning, when he came to inspect the previous night's carnage.

'Get rid of that carrion,' he ordered callously, bending eagerly to lift the angular firing pin and shake it free of sand. He inspected it carefully, then, apparently satisfied, he turned to Travis and Medina, who had limped clumsily along behind him.

'Looks like the cards are finally falling our way,' he crowed, finding it impossible to keep the triumph out of his voice.

Medina shrugged. 'They ain't just gonna stan' up to be shot,' he began uneasily. 'An that Ranger, I tink he is maybe in league wit' the Evil one.' Hurriedly, he crossed himself, checking anxiously over his shoulder as though frightened the entity mentioned might have come to claim his corroded soul.

'Youse sure maybe right,' Travis agreed, eyes rolling. 'If he ain't in league wid the gennleman, he shore got the devil's own luck!'

'You yellow bastards,' Doc sneered, blue eyes hard as adamantine as he grasped the Mexican's collar and

136

fixed him with a cold stare. Medina cringed as the black-dressed killer snarled, 'You'll be jumping at your own shadows next. Medway, or whatever his real name is, is just a man. And I'm going to have the pleasure of letting daylight through him to prove it!'

Dawn had come to the hacienda that morning as well, but the usual activity associated with that time of day was absent, along with most of its inhabitants.

In the big house, however, someone was stirring. Marcia Lopez eased open the heavy door of Wilson's study, gasping in fear as the hinges squeaked a protest. Heart in mouth, she waited, but no one seemed to have stirred and, hardly daring to breathe, she slipped through the opening and moved noiselessly across the room.

Carefully, alert for the least sound, she began to ease open the drawers of the desk, occasionally removing a document or sheaf of papers.

As the pile in front of her grew, she turned impatiently, looking for some sort of container, only to freeze immobile as a voice said gently, 'You really must be careful with those bond certificates, Marcia, my dear. They aren't worth anything if the seal comes off.'

Stiffly, the woman turned, to find a gently smiling Wilson, surrounded by half-a-dozen grinning thugs. The Easterner eased himself down in his wheelchair.

'Tie her into that chair,' he began judiciously, 'then get a rope and some candles. Oh, and leave her legs free, boys,' he finished, the light of appetite flaring briefly in his washed-out eyes.

'What you figger they're doin'?' Sinclair demanded.

'I told you,' Medway answered patiently, 'I can't see from here.' He ducked briskly as a burst of automatic fire interrupted the incessant hammering from below, scything the air above their heads. He risked a quick look over the barricade, pulling back with a dissatisfied shake of his head.

'They've got it pretty well hidden, down in them trees, whatever it is,' Medway said pensively, looking across the mine compound. 'But you can bet your last dollar it ain't nothin' good fer us. And afore we do much else, I figure we better empty that shack,' he finished, voice rising as he pointed at the rickety wooden shed with a hastily scrawled DANGER EXPLOSIVES sign over the door. Almost instantly, struck by a wayward thought, Medway demanded, 'What you got in there? Dynamite?'

'Naw,' Sinclair shook his head. 'Dynamite's tricky stuff in this heat. There's some ammo, not much and a couple kegs o' giant powder. Oh, and some kerosene.'

Medway nodded with some satisfaction. 'Find Señor Negas and Jose. Tell 'em I got a job for them.'

Juan Negas, Sinclair's Juarista corporal, was a white-haired copy of his young son. The two Mexicans listened carefully while Medway explained his plan, then the old man grinned and said, '*Bueno*. We blow all them goddamn bastards to bits.'

Medway nodded and asked, 'Think you can get enough bottles?'

The old man shrugged. 'Sure,' he said, 'There are plenty of empty ones around the place and if there ain't,' – he winked – 'me and my *companeros* will soon fix that.'

'Just how many of your *amigos* might there be still here, exactly?' Medway asked, having heard Sinclair's lurid comments on the number of overnight desertions.

'Eleven, mebbe twelve, *señor*. Don't worry,' Negas senior answered reassuringly, 'the others, they were jus' farmers. Only good to stop bullets. The ones who are left will die before they run.' He stopped on seeing Medway's raised eyebrow. 'Mebbe you don' think greasers can fight,' he finished, voice dangerously soft.

'I don't need no convincin',' Medway assured him, holding up both hands, 'I'm a Texan an' I had some experience o' your people. Like most folks,' he went on bluntly, 'there are some who are liars and thieves and cowards and there are others I've met who would spit in the face o' the devil hisself and call him a liar.'

A smile split Negas' lined face.

'I have also met Texans like that, *señor*,' he offered gently.

Medway grinned back. 'Mebbe so,' he admitted, dropping a hand on the younger Negas' shoulder. 'But take my tip: don't let this one spit too hard!' And he was gone before Jose could think of a suitable retort.

The rest of that long hot day settled down to pot shooting, both sides trying to take advantage of any carelessness on the part of the enemy. There would be a long drawn out wait, sometimes so long that the tension would ooze out of the situation and only the

139

heat and flies and ceaseless chatter of the insects would have any reality. Then suddenly, a shot would ring out and there might be a cry, jerking everybody's mind back to the present. By mid afternoon, the little force behind the barricade had been reduced by a third and still their attackers pecked away at their shelter. There was, however, one compensation: the Gatling gun had ceased.

'I been thinking,' Sinclair offered. 'Where did that bastard Wilson get that gun? I thought you said that Slim and Shorty busted the other two and took the firin' pins? An' why in hell, ain't they still shootin' at us with it?'

'Dunno,' said Medway, obviously answering the last question. 'And they did bust them other two guns.'

'So where—' Sinclair began.

'It's our gun, the one we left at the pass. And I'm guessin' the pin was the original, what I dropped when they killed my horse,' Medway explained. He turned back to study a sudden flurry of activity down the slope.

'But you told me, Shorty picked that pin up,' Sinclair reasoned slowly. 'And if they got it, that means—'

'Slim and Shorty didn't make it.' Medway snarled. 'They musta got caught after they ditched the remuda.' He glared down the slope, then snapped, without looking at his companion, 'Which means there ain't gonna be no last-minute rescues, so we'd better just do the best we can.' Momentarily, the Ranger stiffened, then he said quietly, 'Best you tell the boys to get ready. Looks like they're coming.'

*

Doc hadn't been wasting his time, He had brought two wagons from the hacienda and used the timber from one to build a loopholed wall across the back of the second. Harness and wagon tongue had been modified so that two horses could be hitched to push the vehicle up the slope, with a second, lower wall arranged on either side to offer some protection to the animals and men who would also be required to move the contraption. Finally, the Gatling's ugly snout was pushed through its loophole and the deadly thing was secured in position.

Now, with Doc crouched on the wagon bed and feverishly gripping the two brass Gatling handles, the wagon rumbled slowly out of cover and began its slow climb towards the mine and its little band of stubborn defenders.

Behind the barricades, Medway studied the approaching vehicle as it slowly crept into range and hefted a wine bottle which Jose and his father had previously filled.

'It's a cinch,' he explained to Sinclair, as he passed the big Irishman a similar bottle.

'It's full o' giant powder. You just light the wick, that's soaked in kero, and throw it quick. Simple, huh,' he finished, turning away.

'Yeah, but—' Sinclair began.

'No time for that,' Medway snapped. 'See if you an' some o' the boys can't hit one o' them ponies. That'll sure fix 'em. I'll take care of the gate.' And he was gone before Sinclair could object. Carefully, the sergeant placed his bottle behind a substantial baulk of timber, safe from any stray bullet. With equal care he worked the action of his prized Winchester, checked the round in the chamber and eased up the lever. With the weapon snugly cradled over his arm, he moved cautiously in the direction of the gate. Unless he missed his guess, the Ranger was going to need him. And right soon.

Despite intense firing on the part of the defenders, the wagon, bearing its deadly load, finally managed to creep to within thirty yards of the barrier, from where the machine-gun began pouring a withering hail of lead through the defenders' flimsy protection.

Signalling desperately to the elder Negas, Medway lit the fuse of his home-made grenade and flung it with all his might at the defensive wall.

Arching through the air, the bottle bounced off the timber and, still intact, thudded into the dust, without exploding. For a moment, Medway was stunned into speechlessness, then he snapped, 'Wait, it'll just be a—' As if in mockery of his assertion, the fuse suddenly winked out.

'Well, why in hell—' Medway began.

'Because you need a fuse and a blastin' cap to set off giant powder,' Sinclair interrupted. 'Though o' course, there is another way,' he went on, repeater gliding to his shoulder and firing in the same movement.

Struck by the bullet and positioned now directly under the wagon, the bottle exploded with a vicious snap. Glass tore through the leg of one of the wagon horses, sending it mad with pain and causing it to slew around, exposing its flank.

Instantly, Medway emptied his pistol in the animal's direction and, hit by a lucky bullet, it crumpled, screaming. But the defenders' luck had turned too late.

Even as Doc yelped in fear and leapt to the relative safety of the ground, Travis, eyes staring, screamed, 'Come on! Ain't but a handful o' the white bastards left. Kill 'em! Kill 'em all!'

But Sinclair had foreseen this ending. As the giant Negro tore the flimsy barrier aside, the Irishman was bellowing, 'Fall back! Fall back on the shack.' Unbelievably, through the hell of noise and gunfire, Juan Degas heard and rallying what was left of his Juaristas, began a fighting retreat, volley firing as they went.

For a few bare seconds the attackers wavered and in that time, Sinclair, dragging a reluctant Medway, reached the empty explosive shack. Instantly, Sinclair distributed his men while, risking almost certain death, Medway leaned through the window to yell, 'Juan, get your boys up here now!'

But it was too late. As the old man turned to obey, a stray shot smashed into his skull. Killed instantly, he flopped to the ground, but by now, Medway found himself with troubles of his own.

Even as he made to jerk backwards, away from the questing bullets, his neck was grabbed in a vice-like grip and a deep, feral voice snarled, 'You ain't goin' nowhere, Whitey!' Dragged through the window and powerless in Travis's grip, Medway hammered at his face and body with rapidly weakening fists and feet. From somewhere, through the cloudy, red haze that seemed to surround him, he heard a burst of firing and then Slim's voice was screaming, 'Shorty, there! Gut the bastard!' But the red haze was deepening and Medway slipped gratefully into it, wondering if there might be beer in Paradise, to ease the pain in his throat. Stupid, he told himself, Paradise had everything.

CHAPTER
SEVENTEEN

I might not be the greatest planner in the world, Drago admitted cynically to himself, but there ain't many as good with escape routes.

He'd been far back behind the main assault, well out of the firing line, which, with the arrival of the men from Paesar Querte, had suddenly become too close to the action for comfort. So, he'd purloined a horse and slipped away, heading for the hacienda.

Drago allowed himself a cynical smile. What they had was hardly love but he'd enjoy her company while they spent the money and then . . . Well, she was smart and beautiful and an asset to any business. Any illegal business, that was. Drago lapsed into erotic daydreams while he pushed the borrowed pony hard towards the hacienda and his rendezvous.

Barely half the night had gone as Drago urged his tired mount down the slope into the hidden valley, returning the password of the single sentry as he did so. He left the pony, still saddled and uncared for and, drawing a pistol, slipped silently into the building.

But Marcia wasn't in her room and uncertain what to do, he was about to wake Wilson, when the rising scream of a woman in utmost agony burst upon his ears. Blindly, he began to run, drawing his other Colt without thinking.

'She is dead, *Patron*,' the scar-faced *bandido* leered, wiping his fingers with a grimace of distaste on the mat of hair which crowned the head of what had once been Marcia Lopez. Wilson glanced at the Louis Quinze clock on the table at his elbow, before pursing his lips and shaking his head in disappointment.

'You're slipping, little Julio,' he criticized. 'I thought she'd last at least—' Before Wilson could complete his sentence, the door of the study slammed back against the wall. Drago stood framed in the entrance, guns threatening the room.

Cat-like, he covered the space between him and the thing in the chair.

Looking down at what had been a beautiful, vibrant woman, he seemed unaware of the palpable tension invading the room, which Wilson, unable to bear the sight of the still crouching figure, suddenly broke.

'She was just a whore,' he snapped nervously. 'Get yourself another one in Mexico City, if you're partial to that colour.' For a long moment, it seemed that Drago hadn't heard, then his shoulders slumped and an ice-brittle smile froze his face.

'What'd she do?' he asked softly, apparently unaware that both his Colts were now centred on Wilson's stomach.

'She stole from me. I don't allow that,' Wilson snapped, with more confidence than he was feeling. 'You better remember it.'

Drago nodded absently, then asked irrelevantly, 'Your work, Julio?'

'Si,' the evil-visaged thug shrugged nervously.

'Wish I'd bin here to see it. You're sure an artist.' He raised his head as the sound of several ponies being ridden at speed echoed through the walls.

'Get out, all of you,' Drago ordered, 'and tell anyone whose left to report here in the morning with their guns.' His pistol slanted towards the door as Doc and Jorge Medina staggered through it.

'Looks like we need to have a little talk.' he said, ' 'cause I'm guessin' Medway ain't far behind these yeller rats.'

'Forget Medway,' Doc snapped, all but falling into a chair. 'Last I saw of him, Travis was tearing his throat out.'

'You must be about the luckiest son of a b— gun I ever run into,' Slim assured Medway, as the Ranger groped his way to consciousness.

'Oh no, you lie still,' the little man insisted, as Medway made to rise only to fall back under the combined influences of nausea and a feeling that his throat had been ripped out.

Unable to speak, he signed his concern and Slim nodded reassuringly.

'Be fine in a day or so. But you better fergit any ideas of opry singin' fer a while. Here, take a slug o' this.'

147

'This' felt like kerosene going down, but five minutes later, Medway found himself able to stand and rasp quietly, 'So what happened?'

Slim shrugged. 'Shorty got his sticker in Travis but, like the goddamn idiot he is, didn't finish him. I had to help.' Characteristically, he said nothing about the fight, his empty Colt against Travis's razor-sharp machete, nor the head butt that had smashed the man's nose and knocked him sideways and away, where Shorty's lightning blade finished the job.

He said nothing, but Medway knew his friend, so he dropped a hand on the little man's shoulder and said, 'Thanks Slim. That's another one I owe you an' Shorty.

Like a firework exploding, Slim snapped, 'That goddamn stringbean! Sinclair beat him clean by eight, ten greasers, easy, and now he won't pay up.'

Glad to be back to normal, Medway laughed, clutched his throat and then said hoarsely, 'Find him and the kid. Then round up anyone, cavalry or Mex who can sit a horse. And don't fergit the boys from Paesar Querte.' He looked up at the moon, gauging the passage of the night. 'And Slim,' Medway ordered, as the other turned away, 'don't waste time. If the crippled bastard gets away, someone'll have all this to do again.'

Dawn was barely more than an hour away as the little group on the ridge overlooking the Medina rancho finished their preparations.

'And don't fergit,' Medway finished, 'make sure you got plenty o' cover and cartridges while you're

148

watchin' that front door. I ain't presidin' over no goddamn Alamo here.'

'Yes, Momma,' Shorty responded gravely. 'You want to check ol' Slim's diaper while you're at it?'

'Nope,' Medway stated, grinning despite himself. 'I'm leaving the hard jobs to you. Remember,' he went on, 'you got just one hour to settle the sentries and git down to the house.'

'And don't leave none, Shorty, you damned idiot,' snapped Yance Sumers. 'Not like you an' the runt done at Durango that time!'

'That weren't my fault and you know it, yu damn ol' buzzard,' the tall one snapped, with uncharacteristic peevishness. 'C'mon, Slim.'

'Just make sure you ain't late!' Slim threw over his shoulder and then they were gone, leaving Yance Sumers the object of several speculative glances.

'We was what your Mr Wilson'd call . . . eh . . . business associates,' the old Paesar Querte deputy explained, with a shrug and an uneasy glance at several sets of disbelieving eyes. Abruptly, he snapped, 'I'm gonna check the men.'

'We'd best be movin', kid,' Medway decided, motioning Negas to follow, as the old deputy turned away hurriedly. About to slip into the boulder-strewn undergrowth that flanked the house trail, a grin flitted briefly across his lips as he heard Jake Brady demand, 'And just what kinda business would that ha' bin, Deppity?'

'I don't like it,' Medway whispered. 'Where in hell are the guards? C'mon,' he snapped abruptly, moving silently to his feet and sprinting across to the front corner of the house. Still nothing stirred as the pair silently crossed the veranda and Medway eased open the door.

Suddenly, a whippoorwill called from the corner of a nearby building. Negas stiffened and dropped a hand to his Colt but Medway allowed himself a grim chuckle as he whispered, 'That bird's about six four and totin' a repeater. Come on.'

Gently, the heavy door was silently eased back and the Ranger slipped through the foot wide opening, Negas almost treading on his heels. Medway advanced three paces into the room and crouched in the shadow of a heavy table. He reached back, expecting to find Degas behind him but his hand closed on nothing. Cursing silently, he risked a backward glance only to find the hall was empty.

But only for a moment. Suddenly, a light blazed in the corridor leading to the hall and an instant later, Jorge Medina turned the corner accompanied by two men, both with pistols in their hands.

Medway didn't hesitate. A Colt seemed to leap into his fist as he snapped, 'Rangers here! Drop your—' But he had no time to finish.

As Medina dropped the lamp and bolted, his left side companion swung up his weapon, only to be thrown back against the wall, Medway's first shot lancing into his chest. His companion fared no better, as Medway dropped to the floor, snapping two shots into the second man's body as his assailant's bullet spanged harmlessly off the wall.

Without a thought for his two victims, Medway

threw himself full length, opening his mouth to call a warning. He needn't have bothered. Medina had reached the door and even as he heaved it open, a rifle spoke and he jerked backwards, slumping untidily to the floor.

In seconds, Medway was at his side, Colt slanted down on the big Mexican, But there was no need.

'Gut shot,' Medway sneered into the wide, staring eyes. 'Know how long it takes to die from bein' gut shot, greaser?' he asked conversationally. 'A damn sight longer than it took my wife an' boy when you and your murderin' scum went visitin' at my ranch. Across the border, coupla hundred miles north o' here,' he explained savagely, upon seeing the Mexican's blank expression.

For a moment, Jorges Medina forgot his pain as terror lanced through him.

'B-b-but,' Medina stammered, 'that musta been eight, maybe nine years an' you followed for that long? Please,' he begged incoherently as Medway turned to go, slipping away his pistol as he did so, 'don' leave me. I didn't know. For the love of Christ, help me!'

He deserved it. He deserved to die in the most painful and nauseating way possible for what he had done to Lucy and the boy as well as countless others. He deserved it, Medway told himself even as he turned and his palm snapped back the hammer of his Colt twice. Caught in the head by the heavy bullets, Medina died instantly and for a long moment, Medway cursed his softness. Then, he relaxed. Knowing her, this was how Lucy would have wanted it. His eye caught the fancy spurs, with their rowels of golden dollars on the dead man's heels and he was bending to claim them when two shots close together, shattered the silence.

'Jesus, the kid.' Medway cursed, and turned to run, as gunfire and the thunder of hoofs split the night-time silence.

Revenge makes one forgetful and Medway cursed again, foully, as he turned a corner into the main dining-room of the house, taking in the scene before him at one glance. Negas lay against one wall, gun still clutched in one slim hand while Doc alternately swayed and cursed as the blood dripped from his hand in a steady stream.

The two men jerked up their weapons as one and Medway dodged to one side, desperately trying to line his weapon as Doc's bullet slammed into the plaster, inches away. Smoothly, sure he had won, Medway squeezed the trigger, to be rewarded with a dry click. Instantly, he snapped back the hammer, but to no avail as a slow, vicious smile spread across Doc's unprepossessing features.

'So worried about your little friend you forgot to keep count?' the black-dressed killer sneered. A look of pure, delighted malice spread across his face as he eased back the hammer of his double action Colt. Blood dripping from his injured left hand was the only other sound, but it seemed to Medway to fill the room as Doc said softly, almost matter of factly, 'Goddamn greaser was good. Unfortunately for you, though, not . . . quite . . . good . . . enough.'

Slowly, he lifted the pistol, dragging out the moment, hoping to see fear in the face of this, the only man who had ever played him for a fool, setting him and his precious reputation at nought.

But he was disappointed. Medway only crouched, waiting a last chance, aching to kill this thing, something less than a man, this creature that so much deserved to die. Just too far to risk a leap, Medway tensed as the gun came level, when, suddenly, from behind his tormentor, a shot rang out. Doc shuddered and half turned, trying to look over his shoulder, then, face a stiffening mask of pain and bewilderment, he fell forward and lay without moving,

'I think . . . we . . . could say the goddamn greaser was . . . good enough,' Negas managed softly, as his prized pistol slipped from rapidly weakening fingers. By the time Medway reached him, the young Mexican was dead. Carefully, the Ranger closed the staring eyes.

'*Vayas con Dios,*' Medway mouthed, eyes stinging. 'When you meet ol' Lucifer, you be sure and spit real hard.'

Booted feet sounded on the wood floored passage as an instant later, Shorty burst through the doorway.

'Jim,' he began, then stopped as he found himself looking into the bore of Doc's pistol.

'Ain't you never learned to knock?' Medway demanded irritably as he rose, shoved Doc's weapon into the back strap of his jeans and began to stuff cartridges through the loading gate of his Colt.

'Cashed, huh?' Shorty said, as he swiftly took in the scene. 'Shame about the kid,' he offered.

'Real shame,' Medway agreed. 'He'd've been some kinda man.' Then memory nudged and the Ranger

153

snapped, 'Christ, where's Drago and Wilson?' And as if in answer, the night was split by the thunder of hoofs and the sound of heavy wheels accelerating to full speed. Medway was at the nearby window in a single bound, then he was tearing open the outside door and emptying his Colt into the starlight.

'*Get mounted*!' Medway screamed. 'That bastard Drago's done it again!'

CHAPTER EIGHTEEN

It wasn't until he reached the treacherous slope which led finally to the rim rock and safety, that Drago dared to pull his giant bay to a halt and risk a glance backwards. What he saw was hardly reassuring.

Men were scurrying like ants, desperately slapping saddles on to ponies, while a group of perhaps half a dozen were already mounted and tearing towards the wagon trail up which he had just ridden. That group was enough for Drago.

He jerked the bay's head round, clapped spurs home and thundered up the slope after Wilson's carriage, coming abreast of the leaders and turning in front of them just as Julio, the scar-faced torture expert now turned driver, eased the team and carriage over the last of the slope and on to the flat ground beyond.

This time, it was the Mexican who looked back as Wilson grumbled querulously from the window.

Turning back to his team, as the pursuing riders laboured up the slope a bare 500 yards away, Julio yelled, '*Señor*! Get out of the way! The gringos, they are coming.'

Instead of moving, Drago crossed his hands over the pommel and said, 'See, Julio, she weren't just my woman.' The Mexican looked blank for a moment, then understanding dawned. His hand was closing on the butt of the pistol at his side, when Drago's bullet caught him in the stomach and he fell from the vehicle's box without a sound. A lucky snatch secured the reins of the leaders and Drago half cursed, half dragged them round until they faced the labouring riders, breasting the slope barely a long rifle shot away.

'What are you doing, you goddamn fool!' Wilson screamed, as he attempted to raise the Derringer clutched in a shaking hand. In answer, Drago jerked up a Colt and sent two bullets crashing into the fear-whitened face framed in the window. The banker slumped bonelessly as Drago twisted in the saddle and shouted, 'She was my partner, too, and I allus pay them sort o' debts.'

Ruthlessly, he fired twice over the heads of the leaders and, as the team jerked into a gallop back the way they had come, he emptied his Colt into the figure slumped inside the vehicle.

But this last piece of wanton cruelty proved his undoing. Down the slope, Shorty jerked his rifle to his shoulder and began to throw lead as fast as he could work the action. Hit by one of the tall one's bullets, the bay screamed and collapsed, throwing Drago clear as it did so. For a moment, the outlaw lay stunned, before stumbling to his feet just as Medway, who was

156

leading the mad scramble up the trail, appeared over the rim.

Recognition was instant and mutual, both men reaching for their weapons in a burning desire to kill. Drago's shot cut a furrow in the flank of his enemy's borrowed mount as, a split second later, Medway's bullet sliced into the outlaw's chest.

Screaming in pain, the pony bucked and lunged as Medway fought the maddened little beast, before finally managing to kick loose the stirrups and slip from the saddle.

Swiftly, he moved across to where Drago lay sprawled on the clean white sand, a tiny, trickle of blood defacing the front of his jacket, the only sign of any wound. Medway slipped a hand under the outlaw's shoulders, prior to lifting him and recoiled at the warm, wet stickiness.

Abruptly, Drago's eyes snapped open and he smiled as if understanding the Ranger's disgust.

'Ain't walkin' away from this one,' Drago managed, bright blood decorating his lips as he coughed. 'Wilson,' he went on, 'is the bastard dead?' Gently, Medway nodded and Drago managed weakly, 'He killed the . . . girl. She . . . partner . . . debt paid.' Drago summoned a smile, a shockingly white-faced parody of his usual insolent grin and mumbled, 'We . . . sure . . . found out who . . . was fastest.' With a sudden access of strength, he gripped Medway's hand.

'Want . . . you . . . know . . . Ranger . . . never killed a woman or kid . . . ever . . . or . . . let . . . it be done,' he managed painfully. 'Bluffin' . . . you that time in . . . Wayside. Wanted . . . you to . . .' he began but before he could finish, his head slumped sideways.

And that was how Slim and Shorty found him, kneeling by the body of the man he had sworn to kill. He didn't look up when they approached but as they ranged alongside him, Medway said, 'Need a shovel. Got a buryin' to do.'

'That!' Shorty jerked out, before he could stop himself. Medway looked up and to Slim it seemed that something was gone from his *compañero's* cold brown eyes as the Ranger rose to his feet and said, 'Not "that", *him*. And he earned it.'

Medway made to turn away as Slim said quickly, 'What about the rest of 'em? Down below and all.'

'We cleaned house pretty good,' Medway shrugged. 'Let the Paesar Querte boys take care of it. Me for home,' he finished, and the look in his eyes spoke of places and things far away. 'Home,' he repeated. 'An' Jenny an' l'il Bud.'

As they walked down the slope side by side, Shorty demanded, 'What about us, Slim? What do we do now?' For a moment, his old-time friend and partner glared at him in disgust, then Slim snapped, 'You got that yeller pony Jim liked so much hid good, ain't you?'

'Sure,' the tall one answered with a shrug.

'An' mebbe you figger it wouldn't be worth our while to look over ol' Jorge's remuda, on account of there bein' nothin' there worth keepin'?'

'I . . .' Shorty began, then light dawned. 'Oh,' he finished.

'Oh, is right, Slim snapped. 'Git your pony afore somebody else starts figgerin'.'

'Sure, runt,' came the contented reply.